THE PHOTOGRAPHER

MEIKE ZIERVOGEL grew up in Germany and came to Britain in 1986. Her debut novel *Magda* was shortlisted for the *Guardian*'s Not the Booker prize and nominated as a book of the year 2013 by the *Irish Times, Observer* and *Guardian* readers. Meike's second and third novel, *Clara's Daughter* (2014) and *Kauthar* (2015), were both published to critical acclaim. Meike is the publisher of Peirene Press.

MEIKE ZIERVOGEL

THE
PHOTOGRAPHER

SALT

LONDON

PUBLISHED BY SALT PUBLISHING 2017

2 4 6 8 10 9 7 5 3 1

First published in Great Britain in 2017 by
Salt Publishing Ltd
International House, 24 Holborn Viaduct, London EC1A 2BN United Kingdom

www.saltpublishing.com

Salt Publishing Limited Reg. No. 5293401

A CIP catalogue record for this book is available from the British Library

ISBN 978 1 78463 114 7 (Paperback edition)
ISBN 978 1 78463 115 4 (Electronic edition)

Typeset in Neacademia by Salt Publishing

Printed and bound in Great Britain by Clays Ltd, St Ives plc

To my grandparents:
Heinrich & Lotte
Arnold & Lisbeth

THE PHOTOGRAPHER

PART I: HOME

Child's Play

ONCE UPON A time there was a German town in Pomerania, a medieval fortress with four gates and eight towers. In the middle of the town stood the biggest church in the region, Marienkirche. Our story starts one morning in the early spring of 1920. In an apartment not far from Karowscher Park lives five-year-old Trude. Her mother is a seamstress and her father a carpenter. He fought in the Great War and came home with a wound in his chest and three missing toes.

Trude has woken up early. The birds outside are still asleep. She is kneeling in front of the bed, pulling a little suitcase out from underneath. She unbuckles the belt, lifts the lid and starts to pack. Pants, vests and, her most precious possession, a red nightie with puffed sleeves. Her mother made it but the girl has not worn it yet because she worries that it will crease. Her woollen socks. She doesn't need any outdoor clothes; they won't be much use where she is going. Trude tries to remember the images from the film. The beautiful lady was wearing a lace nightie with wide tulle sleeves, and her shoulders were covered in a delicately knitted shawl with two bobbles at the front. Asta Nielsen – that's the name of the actress. The film is old, her mother said, from before the war. But Trude didn't mind because Asta Nielsen looked like an angel in that shawl. Trude needs something like it, something she can put around her shoulders so she won't get cold while she is sitting in the hospital bed. She has no shawl, but she

3

does have a cardigan. She will drape it around her shoulders like Frau Knopf, who lives in the big villa. What else? Asta Nielsen embroidered while she sat in bed. Trude doesn't like needlework and isn't much good at it either. How about taking a book instead? Her mother could read her stories. After all, she will of course be lying in the bed next to her daughter's. Having a baby in hospital is very chic indeed. Only ladies in the movies have theirs in hospital. And Trude's mother. Trude fetches her fairy-tale book with the big pictures that look like real paintings. And her comb. Then she closes the suitcase and pushes it back under the bed.

She doesn't know what else to do. Wouldn't it be nice if the baby came today? It's Sunday and Sundays are always boring. If the baby came today at least something exciting would happen. Mummy's tummy is already quite big. Mummy and Daddy want a boy. They wanted a boy before, but then Trude came along instead and her father had to go to war. Trude walks into the corridor and stands in front of her parents' bedroom. She doesn't want to be alone any longer. She opens the door and scurries up to her mother's side.

'Mummy,' she whispers.

Agatha opens her eyes.

'Is the baby coming today?'

'Today? No, not today.'

'When is it coming?'

'I don't know, Trude. Babies come when they want to come. Go back to bed. It's too early to get up.'

Agatha closes her eyes again. For a moment Trude looks at her sleeping mother, then she returns to her room. It's lovely and warm underneath the duvet. Her feet have got cold. She curls up, pulls the cover up to her nose and goes back to sleep.

'Where's my mummy?'

Trude is standing at the door to the kitchen.

At the table Frau Silberstiel is sitting with Lotte on her lap, feeding her porridge. Frau Silberstiel lives next door. Mummy says Frau Silberstiel is strange. She is Jewish. But she has a good heart. She always looks after children whose mothers are too young to have them. Lotte is not her real baby either. The parents of the young women give Frau Silberstiel money to look after the babies, Trude's mother says.

'Where is my mummy?' repeats Trude. A funny feeling is creeping into her tummy.

Lotte, on the other hand, is as happy as a lark. She flashes huge smiles at Trude, her face covered in porridge – there is even some stuck on her big forehead. The woman puts another spoonful in front of the toddler's mouth, which opens like that of a little bird, while Lotte's face is still turned towards the door.

'Well done,' Frau Silberstiel coos. Then she looks at Trude. 'Get dressed. I'll make you breakfast.'

'Where is my mummy?' Tears well up in the girl's eyes.

'Your mother had to go to hospital. She'll be back soon.'

Lotte gurgles and laughs, and the porridge runs out of her mouth and down her chin.

'But . . . but,' splutters Trude. Why didn't Mummy wake her up?

The girl turns on her heels, runs into her room, drags out the suitcase from under the bed. There is no time to get dressed. She marches out of the room, along the corridor. She knows what to do. She will get to the hospital on her own.

Her mother has always said that she, Trude, will be the first to hold the baby.

'What are you doing, young lady?' Frau Silberstiel, with Lotte perched on her hip, has appeared at the kitchen door.

Trude is sitting on the floor, putting on her boots. The woman's towering frame does not deter the girl from her task. She tightens the lace of the second boot, stands up, takes her coat from the low hook that her father carved for her in the form of Snow White with a couple of her dwarfs. Frau Silberstiel puts Lotte down on the floor. Trude buttons her coat while she keeps an eye on the fat toddler waddling towards her. Before Trude has time to move, Lotte has wrapped her short arms around her, Trude's, legs. With a forceful movement of her hand, Trude pushes the pest away. Lotte falls to the floor, holding her breath for a moment, flabbergasted. Then she wails.

Without losing any more time, Trude picks up the suitcase and turns to the door. Frau Silberstiel's hand grasps the girl's thin arm, trying to pull her away. But Trude is holding on to the handle with all her might. Dropping the suitcase from her other hand and wrestling herself free from the woman's grip, she pushes down on the handle with both hands. The door's locked! Frau Silberstiel's fingers are already trying to pull the key out of the lock when Trude bends forward and bites. She hears something crunching as her teeth hit bone. Horrified, she opens her mouth. Frau Silberstiel pulls out the key. Trude didn't want to hurt Frau Silberstiel. She just wants to help her mother with the baby in hospital. 'You will help me with the new baby, won't you?' her mother had said. Frau Silberstiel's face is now turning red in rage and pain. Lotte sits behind them on the floor, howling.

'Into your room!' Frau Silberstiel hides the key in her fist, briefly examining the blood-flecked tooth marks on the back of her hand.

Shocked by her own deed, Trude hasn't moved.

'That's enough. Children don't belong in hospitals.' The woman stares angrily at Trude, feeling the throbbing wound on her hand. Frau Weiss has mentioned before what a nuisance her daughter can be. But she, Frau Silberstiel, has never seen it with her own eyes. Until now. She has only ever known Trude as a rather quiet and shy girl.

Trude's head is hanging forward, big tears falling on to her brown, unpolished boots.

'I want to see my mummy,' she sobs.

Suddenly, as if pushed by a force beyond herself, she turns again to the door, kicking and hammering her fist against it.

'Let me out!' The door shakes. 'Let me out!'

Trude screams as loudly as she can, until a hand places itself over her mouth and her feet are lifted off the floor. For a fleeting second, with ferocious determination, the girl keeps hold of the handle, but she is too weak to resist being pulled backwards. She has to let go. Frau Silberstiel puts Trude down, but not for long enough for the girl to understand what is happening to her. The woman forces her arms under Trude's and crosses her forearms in front of the girl's chest, holding Trude tight. She begins to drag her along the corridor.

'Let me go!' the girl screams, trying to throw her body from side to side.

And then. Suddenly. She sees it.

At once she freezes.

The door to her parents' bedroom has swung open: the bed still unmade, the covers lying carelessly crumpled at the

7

bottom, half on the floor. On the mother's side there is a huge bloodstain. Trude has never seen so much blood before. Her mother must have bled to death. What have they done to Trude's mummy?

Frau Silberstiel jostles the girl towards her room. Trude is in such a state of shock that for a few steps she doesn't resist. She is pushed into her room and, before she has time to straighten herself up, the door is pulled shut with a bang and the key turned from the outside.

Trude cowers against the door, her legs pulled in to her chest. She holds on to them tightly. For a while she cries silently, but then she stops. Crying is no use. She has to save herself. And Lotte. Of course she has to save the little girl. Trude is no wicked person who would leave a small child in the hands of a witch. And she's now convinced that Frau Silberstiel is a wicked witch. That's why her mother always says that Frau Silberstiel is strange. Trude is courageous. And her father will come back and rescue them. She only saw blood on her mother's side of the bed. Her mother might be dead and the baby too. No, not the baby. Babies always survive: they scream and breathe and kick. Trude has already seen the baby kicking against her mother's tummy and felt its little heel. It must have hurt. The girl is certain that the baby is alive and her father too. That's how it works in fairy tales. The father always survives, like in Cinderella's story. He's probably burying the mother. And soon a beautiful hazel bush will grow on her mother's grave. Trude looks just like Cinderella in the picture in her book. And now she is cowering against the door, lonely and forsaken, just like Cinderella. Abandoned by everyone and kicked by the wicked Frau Silberstiel. But Trude will survive.

After all, Cinderella survived and married a beautiful prince.

The girl enjoys the new role. She tousles her hair and lies down on her side, pushing her back up against the door and pulling her legs in tight to her chest. A cold draught comes through the bottom of the door. It penetrates the coat that she is still wearing. Cinderella must have felt just like this while lying in the cold ashes.

The front door opens, then slams shut; the key is turned from the outside. Trude can hear Frau Silberstiel's steps on the wooden stairs. After that, total silence.

Trude has turned to stone. She has never ever in her entire life lain that still.

Something has happened. Frau Silberstiel has murdered Lotte. And she will return to get Trude.

Frau Silberstiel has killed everyone: her mother, the baby and Lotte too. She eats little children. In fact, that's why she looks after them. Only Trude and her father are still alive. But where is Daddy? Carefully, so as not to make any scraping noise, she pulls her knees a few centimetres higher.

A horse neighs in the street below. Terrified, Trude halts mid-movement. But nothing else happens.

The draught from under the door has got worse. The bed. She has to get into bed. And hide beneath the blanket. Like in a cave. She'll be safe there. When Trude dreams of ghosts and monsters at night, she knows she'll be safe as long as she stays totally hidden. Sometimes the monsters are everywhere, but they can't get to her as long as she stays beneath the duvet. The trick, however, is that nothing, absolutely nothing, is allowed to show, not a corner of her nightie, not a single hair, not a toe. But now the bed seems so far away. At the other end of

9

the room. And she doesn't dare look too closely in case the monsters are lurking beneath it.

The danger is not only prowling outside the room but has already entered it. Because Frau Silberstiel is a witch and witches practise black magic, Frau Silberstiel or Frau Silberstiel's helper might already be under the bed. And it's only because Trude hasn't moved yet that they don't realize she is here. She tries to make herself even smaller by pulling in her tummy, to make herself blend in with the floor or the door. That's probably also why Frau Silberstiel hasn't killed her after murdering Lotte. Witches always have weak eyesight and a bad memory, so she has simply forgotten that Trude is here.

Then, without any further thought, Trude jumps to her feet, runs across the room, throws herself into bed, pulls the duvet over her head, holding on tightly from the inside. She curls up. With her free hand she smooths her hair to ensure that not a single strand escapes. She pulls her coat tighter around her body and her knees higher and lowers her chin on to them. She has turned into a little ball, closed within itself so that evil can no longer touch her or harm her.

The fear starts to evaporate. But not for long. As it returns, Trude focuses all her energy on keeping her little ball of safety intact, pushing her chin as hard as possible against her knees, while trying not to breathe, so that the up and down movement of the cover doesn't betray her.

When the mattress shakes, she screams. She screams so loudly that she can't hear anything else. She holds her hands over her ears, presses her eyes shut. Only her mouth stays wide open. Whatever might happen now, she doesn't want to know. She kicks. She notices the duvet slipping off her body. The cold embraces her. Then she feels a hand on her hips and she screams even more loudly, and presses her hands even harder against her ears, squeezes her eyes shut even tighter, kicks more ferociously and throws her head wildly from side to side. Another hand takes hold of her wrist, wants to pull the hand away from her ear. Never! She will not allow that to happen. If the monster wants to gobble her up, tear her apart, so be it, but she will not watch that happening to herself. Never! The hand keeps hold of Trude's wrist. It is a strong hand. Eventually, she can no longer stop her hand being removed from her ear.

'Trude, you are dreaming. Calm down.'

She hears the words, but she doesn't want to understand them.

'Trude!'

The voice is stronger now, more determined. She recognizes it. She stops kicking, suddenly lying motionless. Her eyes are still shut but she is no longer screaming. The hand releases her wrist and she can press her palms against her ears again. Which she does, but no longer as firmly. They rest loosely at the side of her face.

She opens her eyes.

'Mummy.'

In one movement she sits up and throws both arms around her mother's neck.

For a moment Agatha sits immobile on the edge of her daughter's bed, then she too hugs the girl tightly. Trude weeps on her mother's shoulder. Finally there is no need to hold back her tears any longer.

'You had a bad dream.'

Trude lifts her head, wiping her nose with the back of her hand. She shakes her head, sobbing: 'No, I didn't dream.

Frau Silberstiel . . . Frau Silberstiel was really mean . . . and
. . . and . . .' She searches for words to express the horror of
what has happened. Her mother is clearly still alive. But what
about the baby?

'I asked Frau Silberstiel to look after you.'

Trude shakes her head. Then her glance falls on her mother's tummy. The tummy is still there but it looks somehow
different. Smaller.

'She . . . she . . .'

'Frau Silberstiel had to shut you in your room because you
wanted to run away.'

Doesn't her mother understand? Doesn't she know? Trude
edges away, pressing herself against the wall but keeping her
eyes firmly on the funny-looking tummy. Her mother, Trude
now notices, doesn't look normal either. She looks like a ghost.
So pale.

'Is the baby still in there?'

Her mother shakes her head.

'Where is the baby?' Trude's tone is defiant. She can't allow
herself to show fear. Something is not right. 'There was a lot
of blood,' she adds.

'It's all clean now. And the baby is next door.'

Her mother doesn't look happy about the baby at all.

'Did Frau Silberstiel do that?'

'What? Clean up?'

The girl shakes her head. 'No. Make you bleed.'

'Of course not.'

Her mother's voice sounds strange. As if she isn't telling
the truth.

'I still think Frau Silberstiel is mean.'

'Trude, listen to me. Frau Silberstiel is not mean. She is

a kind woman. I've explained to her that you are a bit of a scaredy-cat and that your imagination runs wild. She understands, but you will never repeat the performance from this morning. Is that clear?'

Trude nods. Secretly, however, she decides to watch Frau Silberstiel closely from now on. Because only she knows what Frau Silberstiel is really like.

Every now and again Trude nods, smiles, moves her lips as if she is saying something, responding to something. As if she is holding a conversation. But not a word can be heard. She leans forward, pretending to serve tea, pouring it from a delicate white china pot into an even more delicate china cup. She picks up the air-saucer and guides her air-cup to her mouth, holding the handle between thumb and index finger with her little finger out straight. She is an elegant lady. She is wearing her red nightie with the puffed sleeves. They are having a picnic. She is chatting to a prince, whose horse is tied up by a tree. The prince is in love with her. She, too, is in love with the prince. Soon they will get married. And then they will live happily ever after, smiling at each other like the dancer dressed as a prince and the beautiful ballerina in the photograph that her friend Ilse had given her. 'From Paris,' Ilse told Trude. Ilse's uncle visited Paris. Trude has hidden the photograph in a metal box behind the chicken coop at the bottom of the garden. It's her secret.

From the corner of her eye Trude is watching her mother, who is now leaving her sewing and walking over to the wooden crib where the baby lay for a few days. Her mother often walks over to the crib, kneels down beside it and rocks it gently, humming a song – a song that Trude doesn't know. A lovely, sad song only for the dead baby. Her mother crouches by the empty crib for a long time. In the meantime the prince has mounted his horse again. He's approaching Trude, who is still sitting on the floor under the big table in her mother's sewing room, and from his horse he bends down towards her and offers her his hand. Trude doesn't move, waiting for her mother to return to her sewing work. Finally her mother gets up. She holds her arms as if carrrying a baby and she sits on the sofa. For the few days that the baby, the real baby, was there, it was always asleep. 'Not like you, Trude. You used to scream until you turned blue in the face.' Her mother is now opening the buttons of her blouse. She puts a little bowl into her lap, leans forward and squeezes the milk out. Then she leans back and closes her eyes. When the baby used to suck on her mother's breast, the sucking noise travelled right across the room, to underneath the table where Trude was sitting. It made a lot of noise. Trude is never allowed to make such a noise at mealtimes. But no one seemed to mind with her little brother. 'He is such a good boy,' Trude's mother would say. 'He sleeps and drinks and doesn't cause any trouble. With you, Trude, it was a different story.'

Trude turns away from the sight of her mother. The prince is still holding out his hand. The girl smiles and places her hand in his. In one big sweep he lifts her up on to his horse and sets her down in front of him. But not straddled across, like men and farmers and poor people; no, like a princess, with both legs to one side. She feels his strong arms encircling her from the left and the right, so that he can hold the reins in front of her.

The Arrival of the Prince

A REAL PRINCE did eventually arrive in Trude's life, but it took a few years. In the meantime, her father died of the war wound in his chest and her mother became a respected seamstress, counting the wives of town notables such as lawyers and doctors among her clients.

So, one sunny Sunday afternoon shortly after her eighteenth birthday, Trude was strolling along Nightingale Walk when, from afar, she spotted a young man sitting on a bench beneath the old maple tree.

Albert is smoking a cigarette. His camera is on the tripod next to him. Business has been good today. Lots of young families out for a Sunday stroll enjoy having their picture taken. He will have to work through the night to develop all the photographs in time. Most customers want them as quickly as possible.

He takes another drag and then leans back, his face turned upwards. Perfect smoke rings escape slowly from his mouth.

Taking photographs of families is pretty straightforward – they all look the same, want to look the same. Albert bends forward and spits out some strands of tobacco that have got caught between his teeth. The husband with a slight paunch, hat and walking stick, tall and upright, staring proudly and unsmilingly into the camera. Some are sporting the ridiculous moustache of this Hitler. Next to the man his wife, sometimes with her arm in his but very often not, smiling faintly, as if not sure or perhaps even slightly unhappy, meek really, and then two or three children, standing like a row of Russian dolls, in their Sunday best, well behaved, polished, indistinguishable. Albert brings the cigarette up to his mouth again. Easy money. That's what counts. And he never shows his disdain in front of his customers. The trick is to find something interesting – there is always something interesting with everyone: a single curl of hair along the side of a woman's neck; the Adam's apple jumping hectically up and down in a man's throat as if wanting to scream out loud; the barely contained mischievous twinkle in a child's eye. And soon he'll be off anyway. Berlin, Paris, Rome, New York. It's in the magazine world where he will make his mark. Speed, combined with his technical know-how and good eye, has become his trademark. *Albert – your speedy photographer*, announces the sign next to him.

'Well, well, then, where is our speedy photographer? Fast asleep!'

A light, laughing, mocking woman's voice. Albert's gaze travels from the two pairs of women's shoes that have stopped in front of his bench, up slender legs to two fetching female bodies, arm in arm, rocking slightly in unison from side to side. Red lips, bright eyes, one with a blonde Eton crop, the other dark-haired.

'If Albert is quick enough, he may take our picture.' The blonde one throws him a provocative glance. It was she who had first spoken.

'Trude!' The other gives her friend a playful nudge on the hips. 'He's a stranger. If your mother found out!'

The blonde rolls her eyes. Then she covertly bows towards Albert. 'Young man, you have to excuse us. I received my first pay packet on Friday and so my friend and I have been celebrating this afternoon at Café Reimers with a couple of glasses of Sekt.'

Albert draws on his cigarette. The blonde looks cute. The dark-haired one too. In fact, both are very good-looking. But the blonde has a certain *je ne sais quoi*. A bit of bite, but warmth as well, both at the same time, like the early autumn weather today. He drops his cigarette butt to the ground, stands up and steps on it while looking straight into the blonde's blue eyes.

'I'm happy to take a picture of the two ladies. But what will you offer in return?'

Without hesitation, the blonde leans towards him, goes up on tiptoes and breathes into his face: 'A kiss.' She smells wonderful. Of roasted chestnuts.

Her friend pulls her arm. 'Trude, let's go.' Then, with a glance towards Albert: 'I'm sorry for my friend's behaviour. We have to go.'

She turns away, trying to drag Trude with her. But Trude resists, freeing her arm and keeping her eyes firmly on Albert's face. She lifts her hand and points with her index finger. 'Only one. One little kiss, that's what you are going to get from me, if you photograph my friend and me.'

Albert receives his payment behind the thick old tree trunk. The families with their children have long gone home. The sun is setting. The dark-haired one is acting as a lookout in the twilight – just in case. Trude's full, soft lips on his. For a moment she doesn't move. Will she pull back immediately? Lightly, he places his right hand on her hip; the left hand remains stretched out above her head, resting against the tree trunk. Her lips stay on his. Carefully he increases the pressure of his fingertips on her hip. Will she come closer? Her body doesn't indicate any resistance, but neither of them moves. Instead her lips begin to part and he feels her tongue. So briefly, so quickly, he almost misses it. His brain hardly registers it, but his body reacts. She, however, has already stepped aside.

'There you go, young man. I hope you enjoyed it.'

She laughs and disappears around the tree, back on to the path, where she seizes her friend's hand. Albert needs a few moments to gather his wits. Then he hurries after them, stumbling over his own feet and nearly falling, which amuses the young ladies mightily and makes him blush. He pulls out his business card.

'The photograph will be ready tomorrow morning. You can pick it up whenever you want.' Albert catches Trude's eye one more time.

When she walked into the shop three evenings later – she had decided to leave him on tenterhooks just for a bit – his heart, which had been thumping in his chest in hopeful, jittery anticipation ever since the kiss, actually stopped for a few beats. Then he put on his hat and offered the beautiful young woman his arm. They strolled along the river and he took her for dinner at Hotel Schöne Aussicht and afterwards to Hugo's, on the shore of the Madüsee, where his friend Max played with his band. There Albert discovered that Trude was the best dancer he had ever held in his arms. And that settled it for him. What a lucky man he was! And he whispered into her ear, 'Will you come with me to Berlin and Paris and Rome and New York?' His breath in her ear tickled and she giggled and said, 'Yes.' And he swung her around and her feet lifted off the ground. With music in their ears and its rhythm in their blood, and the taste of wine and whisky in their mouths, they rowed out on to the lake as the night sky began to lift.

A Boy from the Gutter

'DID YOU GET it from that boy?' asks Agatha.

They are sitting at the big wooden table in the sewing room. A red dress is lying in Agatha's lap. She is holding a small, wide-open pair of scissors in her right hand, pushing the pointed blade underneath a stitch, then gently pulling the thread out. She repeats the action with every stitch of the seam along the back of the dress. Her movements are quick and confident. She doesn't need to concentrate much, feeling the stitches with her thumbnail. Meanwhile, the hands of her eighteen-year-old daughter lie idly on the table. One next to the other; elegant, smooth young hands. A new ring sparkles on the left fourth finger – a gold ring with a small diamond.

When Trude doesn't reply, Agatha interrupts her work and places the scissors and dress on the table. She rises to her feet, goes to the window and shuts it. As Agatha sits down again, their eyes meet briefly, unintentionally, before Agatha's gaze returns to the ring. Trude straightens her back.

'Cocotte!' hisses Agatha.

Trude lifts an eyebrow, but her lips remain a tight thin line.

'You should not keep company with such men.'

'You don't know him at all.' Trude has not yet introduced Albert to her mother.

'Two weeks ago I met Frau Strade in the Blumenstrasse. She asked after your health, since apparently you have missed a few days of work recently.'

Trude is in her first year of a secretarial apprenticeship with Dr Strade's law firm.

'What did you say?'

'I did not expose your lie, if that's what you want to know. I've hinted at your weak chest. But after meeting Frau Strade, I made my own enquiries. Eventually I decided to get a better look at this young man myself. I went to the Rathausplatz, where he stands with his camera, pretending to take photos while in actual fact he flirts with any young woman who crosses his path.'

'He works as a photographer. Taking pictures is his job.'

'He's from the gutter. His father was a drinker, before he disappeared without trace. The mother didn't waste any tears or time and spread her legs for the next man.'

'Watch your tongue.'

'He's not the right company for you.'

'Albert is different. He works hard.'

'He left school when he was eleven. He's a crook.'

'He knows a few queer fish. But he isn't like them.'

'I don't want my daughter to end up like her grandmother.'

Agatha is the illegitimate child of a Polish maid and the son of an East Prussian estate owner. The East Prussian estate owner's son could not resist the innocent beauty of a young Polish maid who didn't speak a word of German. Nine months later Agatha was born in the byre among the cows. The estate owner's son gave the maid a little bag of coins and she and her baby moved on to the next village where she found a new job and a German husband, forty-year-old, one-armed Wilhelm. The Polish maid didn't love the bad-tempered man and never stopped complaining to her daughter about the bad hand life had dealt her.

'Your grandmother was stupid. And look what became of her. Noble blood runs in our veins. Your father, God rest his soul, and I worked hard and have achieved a lot. We no longer live in a dirty village somewhere in the sticks. We live in an apartment with lovely furniture and china. We sent you to middle school and I found you an apprenticeship, despite the hard times. And now you want to throw everything away and travel with a boy from the gutter. To take pictures. No, I won't let that happen. You will stay here, my daughter. And tomorrow I will visit Dr Strade and beg forgiveness for your absence and explain about your poor health and the headaches that cause you to make rash decisions.' Agatha pauses for a moment. 'And regarding this Albert, if you must go dancing with him, do. But do not skip work again, or come home late. This boy is bad news, Trude, and I will not watch my daughter rush headlong into disaster.'

While her mother spoke, Trude did not bat an eyelid. Now she lowers her head. A smile flickers across her lips.

The next morning she is gone.

The Magician

SHE HAS A lot to do. Clients coming and going, and then there is Emma, the girl who helps her. And so during the day Agatha has to keep up a façade. But at night the loneliness grabs her and shakes her about and kicks her and chokes her. Until one day she realizes it has defeated her, wrung her out like a piece of wet cloth and hung her up on a hook in the kitchen. Not even the sewing room. And there she hangs, hooked by the collar of her grey frock. She gave birth to Trude during the war all on her own and looked after her and cared for her. While Otto always wanted a boy, she had always had dreams and aspirations for her daughter. Trude would study and become a famous professor, or a doctor or a lawyer. Like a man. Instead, her daughter fell for the wrong man. And now Trude believes she has no need of her mother – her, Agatha – any longer. And she has simply hung her up on a hook like an old frock. How dare she! The sudden anger that Agatha feels towards her daughter does her good.

She jumps up from the kitchen table, where she has been sitting all these nights, too exhausted to go to bed. And even while still scurrying along the corridor she begins to unbutton the front of her grey frock. It smells. She must have been wearing it for days. Emma must have noticed. The clients must have noticed. When she reaches the last two buttons, she simply rips it open. The buttons fly off and fall to the ground. Liberated, Agatha lets the frock drop to the floor and removes her underwear as she steps into the sewing room. Before she switches on the light she pulls the heavy curtains shut. Then she tips on to the floor all the scraps of fabric that she keeps in the big box. She begins to look for the largest pieces. She stands up and holds them to her naked body, studying herself in the mirror. She doesn't look at her face. With clients too, when they try on the clothes or when they arrive with some fabric, she never pays attention to their faces. She doesn't even look at their bodies, in the sense that these are individual bodies. She surveys the body as a shape, as something that is a necessary part of her work. Without a body she couldn't make clothes. Agatha's goal is always to transform. To transform the piece of material and transform the body in order to create fusion between the two. She's an alchemist. A magician.

She bends down again, rummaging through the material. She then sits back on her feet and laughs out loud. She hasn't laughed since Trude left. It's time to work some magic on herself. She leans forward once more and picks up the smallest pieces. For a moment she stands staring at the bundle in her hand. She wants to fix them to her skin. But how? She puts them on the table and undoes her hair. It falls heavy and full down her back. She ties one scrap after the other into her hair. Then she takes the bigger pieces, sits down at the machine and stitches them together in a rectangular shape in whatever order she picks them up. She cuts a hole in the middle so she can pull the cloth over her head. It comes to just above the knee and looks like the tunics that the Romans used to wear.

Agatha contemplates the apparition in the mirror. The outfit requires a belt. Once again she rummages through the fabric, but then her eye falls on the frock that is still lying in the corridor. She rips it apart, tears off a thick strip and ties it round her waist.

She likes what she sees in the mirror. It makes her smile. She puts a finger against the glass and strokes her reflection's red cheek. Its eyes are shining. She takes a step back and continues looking at herself. The only things that are now missing are a spear and a shield. Again she smiles, tipping her head to the side. The spear and the shield must have come into her mind when she thought of the Roman tunic. But that's what's needed. There's no way round it. It's like a client's dress that is nearly perfect but requires just a tiny adjustment around the collar – where the edges, say, are a few millimetres too high. So often the women can't see what Agatha means, and sometimes they are in a hurry; but she can't let them go, because the smallest imperfection prevents the fusion from taking place – the fusion that will lead to the transformation. And for her, now, she knows that until she finds a spear and a shield she will never become whoever or whatever she's meant to be at this very moment. She walks into the kitchen and fetches the biggest lid she can find, from the pot in which she boils her knickers.

She stands with the broom in her left hand and the lid in her right in front of the mirror. Frankly, it looks a bit silly. It's the broom that is wrong.

She fastens the big kitchen knife to the handle. That doesn't look right either. Maybe she should carve a pointed end.

Then she stands in full gear with spear and shield and red lips and cloth strips in her hair and rag tunic covering her body.

And now Agatha finally looks at herself. She is perfect. Yes, of course, and ridiculous too. She hasn't gone mad. And she turns towards the room and points the spear at the sewing machine, the scraps of material and the reels of thread, and at the three dresses for customers that she's currently working on. And this is her kingdom and in it she rules and in it she makes things happen. She's a magician and she casts her spell. She points the spear towards the window and sends a good spell out towards Trude. To protect her. To bring her daughter home safely.

The spell worked. While the young couple travelled across Europe, Trude wrote to her mother each week. Albert photographed, and his young wife developed the images and kept the books. Their work was published in magazines and newspapers in Berlin, Hamburg, Munich, Paris and Rome.

But eventually Trude persuaded Albert to return. Her guilt at leaving her mother had increased steadily and Albert and Trude had saved enough money to open up their own studio.

They rented an apartment on the other side of Karowscher Park, Peter was born and for a while even Agatha put her doubts about Albert to one side. Not for long, mind. As the next war began to rage, she once more became convinced that she had been right about her son-in-law from the beginning. All the evidence pointed that way. Albert was bad news.

And so Agatha conspired to sort out the situation once and for all.

But first she needed help.

The Exchange

P ETER IS CREEPING along the corridor on tiptoes. His sneaking technique resembles a polished art form, practised to perfection many times. After each step he halts. For two reasons: to check if the normal background sounds have changed, and then to wait until any noise he might have caused himself – such as his breathing, or the scraping of his big toe along the floor – has subsided. Even though he tries to breathe normally and without making a sound, he can't be sure that he really is that quiet. His heart beats so loudly that in his ear it drowns out all the other sounds that emanate from him. Of course, no one is able to hear his heart beating, but they can hear other noises he might make. Especially his mother, who has very good ears.

The boy is standing on a wide step, his right foot about half a metre ahead of the left. Waiting.

Eventually he dares to make the next move. He now places his left foot as far as possible in front without losing his balance. Bodily control is vital, and he cannot allow his foot to thump down on the floor. He wobbles for a second but doesn't topple over. Once again, he waits, listens. Another step. If he were ever caught midway along the corridor it would not be a disaster. He'd say he couldn't sleep. There is no danger here. The dangerous part lies further ahead. There it will be important that no one catches him. And so far no one ever has.

Finally Peter reaches the mirror and the little dresser. He

ventures to take one last big step, leaning his upper body forward and peeping through the gap by the sitting-room door, which stands ajar. His parents are sitting at the table. The white tablecloth is pushed aside. In front of his mother lie a lot of banknotes. She is writing numbers in a book. 'Doing the shop accounts,' she calls it. The radio, too, is on the table. His father is inserting a little wire through the back panel.

Peter pulls his head back and comes to a halt on both feet in front of the dresser. Without hesitation he slides his hand inside his mother's handbag and lifts out a thin black leather wallet. He makes sure that he's not touching or disturbing anything else inside the bag. He's not allowed to change the order of things, and he also needs to take care that the coins in his mother's purse don't clink together. He puts the wallet next to the bag. His mother keeps her own banknotes in this wallet. It is the money she uses for buying groceries and when Peter needs new shoes or when she has to pay Frau Meier for doing the cleaning. The edges of the notes glide along his fingertips. Ten-mark notes, twenty-mark notes, fifty-mark notes and sometimes even a hundred-mark note. A man is speaking on the radio. The music hasn't yet started. Good. Quickly Peter lifts his pyjama top. Underneath it he has tied a long black shoelace around his belly. In front of his belly button, a ten-mark note sticks to his skin.

Today he will do a big exchange, not merely five for ten. Carefully he pushes his ten-mark note among the ten-mark notes in the wallet. Before he pulls out a twenty-mark note, he double-checks that there are at least five twenty-mark notes. If there are fewer, he won't take one. His mother might notice. But luckily there are five. After all, what is important is that the number of notes doesn't change. So, if his mother notices anything, she will think she has miscounted. Peter's exchange technique has so far always worked.

With dexterous fingers, he pushes the twenty-mark note between shoelace and soft warm skin, lowers the pyjama top and returns the black wallet to exactly the same spot inside the bag where it had been before. For a few seconds he pricks up his ears in the direction of the sitting room. Then he turns and, more quickly than before but still on tiptoes and without stopping, he scurries back to his room. At the chest of drawers he pulls the note from underneath his pyjamas, folds it and pushes it into his white porcelain piggy bank; the note drops into the dark piggy belly. Peter breathes a sigh of relief. Now no evidence remains of what he has just done. The money has disappeared inside his piggy bank. He quickly calculates in his head how much he's already got. It must be nearly sixty marks now. He started with the ten he found in the street. Initially he wanted to tell his mother, but then he realized that this could be the first step towards getting enough money to buy his own boxing gloves. Peter wants to become a boxer like Max Schmeling, but his dad doesn't like boxing, and doesn't like the war either. He doesn't like anything to do with fighting, he says. Luckily Peter's teacher, Herr Friedrichs, likes both – boxing and the war – and takes the boys to the barracks when the soldiers hold boxing competitions there. Herr Friedrichs's son is a boxer who is away fighing in the war, and Herr Friedrichs is very proud of him.

Peter removes the shoelace and fetches his boot. Standing at the window, he threads the lace back in.

The music is starting up from the radio. It's very faint because his parents don't want their neighbours to know.

Usually he would now go to bed, but today he has an errand to run for his grandmother.

They were exchanging secrets, Peter and his grandmother. It's a game they sometimes play: who knows a better secret? This time Grandma started. She told Peter that when she was younger she loved dressing up and she showed him a patchwork costume she once made for herself. 'But you are not allowed to tell your mother,' she said with a stern face. Peter agreed that that was a good secret. Still, he wanted to win. His best secret is, of course, the note-exchange business, but he can't tell anyone about that. So he told Omi about the radio that his parents hide in the wardrobe and only listen to late at night. Clearly his parents don't want people to know about that radio – why else would they hide it? But surely they don't mind Omi knowing. She knows everything about their family anyway. They hide it in the wardrobe in their bedroom; Peter hears the squeaking of the doors before the hissing and crackling come from the sitting room. It must be special because they have another radio that lives in the sitting room and they all listen to at the weekend.

His grandmother acknowledged that the hidden radio was a first-class secret and declared Peter the winner of the game. They decided that the radio now constitutes their main shared secret, their special secret, and neither Grandma nor Peter is allowed to mention it to anyone. But Omi wants to know more about the radio and the song that Peter sang for her, because he couldn't remember all the words.

That's why today Peter is scuttling back down the corridor. His heart doesn't beat as loudly and he doesn't stop after each step. Still, he tries to be as quiet as a mouse.

His parents have stood up. His father has put an arm around his mother's waist and drawn her close. Their other two hands are touching in mid-air. His mother's cheek is resting against his father's. They both have their eyes shut and are moving with the rhythm of the music from one leg to the other, turning slowly on the spot. His father whispers something into his mother's ear. She giggles. His father draws the mother even closer.

Very, very quietly, Peter begins to hum along. *Der Führer ist ein Schinder, das seh'n wir hier genau. The Führer is a tyrant, we can see this very well.* It's always the same song. *Zu Waisen macht er Kinder, zur Witwe jede Frau. He turns children into orphans and women into widows.* Whenever his parents listen to the radio at night. *Und wer an allem Schuld ist, den will ich an der Laterne sehen. Hängt ihn an die Laterne. Deine Lili Marleen. He is guilty through and through, so hang him from the lamppost. Hang him from the lamppost. Your own Lili Marleen.*

Later on in bed, Peter tries to imagine what the Führer hanging from a street light would look like. With a thick rope around his neck and his tongue sticking out of his mouth and swaying from side to side. Like Reverend Lorenz, who hanged himself from the old lime tree on the Adolf-Hitler-Platz. Peter was waiting outside the butcher's shop for his mother when he saw the Reverend walking across the square with a stepladder under his arm. It all happened very quickly: by the time the Reverend had kicked the ladder away and was dangling in the tree, his mother had already grabbed his arm and was pulling him into a side street. But the next day his friend Johann Windrose, who sits next to him at school and who was able to get a better look at the dead Reverend, told him about the open mouth and the tongue.

Peter snickers and pulls his duvet up to his nose to stifle the sound. The Führer would look very silly indeed with his tongue sticking out and swaying forlorn in the wind. And he wouldn't be able to shout any longer.

Agatha's Errand

AGATHA FASTENS HER hat with the big pin. She slips into her long brown coat. Quickly, she checks herself over in the mirror. Any marks? Or a hole that she might have torn accidentally? No. She looks clean and tidy.

She picks up her handbag and hangs it over her arm, then pulls the heavy oak door of the apartment shut. The polished wooden stairs creak beneath her feet. She holds on to the banister tightly so as not to slip. She is wearing her best boots with the little buckles. Children's noise from the Silberstiels' apartment meets her on the half-landing. Loud shrieks and squeals. The woman shakes her head disapprovingly. Even though the Krafts are a decent, respectable family – he works for the Wehrmacht and she is a young, strapping blonde – their children are not turning out well. Four boys, between the ages of one and six. They never sit still and spend their days running wild. Terrible. In that respect the Silberstiels, with their little retarded daughter, were bliss. But they left in '36 and for a long time their apartment stood empty. Personally, Agatha never had a grudge against the Silberstiels. They were nice people. Probably a bit old to have a child of their own, though. Frau Silberstiel must have been nearly forty when she gave birth to Sophie. Well . . . God has his ways.

Agatha sighs. She steps on to the pavement, taking care to close the gate to the yard quietly behind her. She doesn't want any nosy neighbours noticing that she is out on an errand this early in the morning. It's a beautiful morning. No clouds in the sky. And for a while the only sound comes from above, where the swallows are nesting underneath the gabled roofs. A lorry approaches from behind. Hollow faces stare out at her from the back. If only they'd close the tarpaulin when transporting the foreign prisoners from the nearby camp through town. A small group of six men in uniform, two to each row, march past her with clicking heels. Agatha presses herself against a house wall. The first five men look down and pay her no attention. The last one, however, scrutinizes her unashamedly, looking her up and down. She doesn't avoid his gaze, returning it defiantly. Let him stare and wonder about her olive skin, her dark brown eyes. A couple of years ago, before her black hair turned prematurely grey, the hassle she had to put up with was much worse. Now her grey hair makes her look older than she is. And that's fine. At least it prevents these boys turning cheeky. Eventually this one too averts his eyes.

Agatha turns into Radestrasse and stops in front of the milliner's. She has put a bit of money aside, keeping it in the little porcelain box with the roses that she hides under the leftover scraps of material. The hat will serve as a consolation for Trude, even though Agatha is sure that her daughter will eventually understand that what she, Agatha, is about to do is for Trude's own good. And for Peter's good. *Der Führer ist ein Schinder.* When she heard her little grandson hum these words, her heart stopped. *Hang him from the lamppost* Of course people listen to the Black Radio. But no one knows who they are and they don't listen in front of their children. Such imprudent behaviour. That's why she invented the game of exchanging secrets with Peter. She had to make sure that Albert was indeed listening to the Black Radio. And now she is certain.

Agatha has to act quickly if she wants to save her daughter and grandson.

She enters the police station, shows her identity card. A young woman leads her into a room where a small, thin man is sitting behind a big desk. It's difficult to gauge his age. He is half bald. He could be fifty, though perhaps he is much younger. She is shown to a chair a couple of metres in front of the desk. The man is busy inserting a new sheet of paper into his typewriter. His tongue presses nervously against the inside of his right cheek. He has not yet looked up. The young woman takes Agatha's identity card from her hand without saying a word, walks over to the desk and puts it next to the typewriter. The man pulls a white handkerchief from his trouser pocket, holds it in front of his mouth and nose, coughs and then keeps it there while the other hand flicks the card over. He pushes it to the edge of the desk. Only when the secretary has picked it up again does he remove the handkerchief from his mouth. He folds it into a neat little square, then slides it into his pocket. Agatha is now holding her card again in her lap, clasping it with both hands. She realizes that she is clinging to it and releases her grip so that one hand rests casually on top of the other. Her feet are placed neatly side by side.

When the man finally looks at her, she decides that it would appear more decent if she were to lower her gaze. Also, she doesn't like the way his mouth distorts while his tongue plays with his cheek.

'Name!'

He could have taken it from her card, she thinks, but replies calmly, 'Agatha Weiss.'

The typewriter begins to pound. Agatha looks up. The man thumps the keys with his two bony middle fingers. Drops of sweat cover his forehead. Agatha thinks about the clear blue sky and is looking forward to finishing her task in this room.

'Born!'

'16 February 1896.'

'Where?!' The man tears his eyes from the typewriter and glares at Agatha furiously. 'When I say "Born" I don't just mean the date,' he shouts, 'but also the place. Is that clear?'

Agatha doesn't lower her gaze this time. She isn't afraid of shouting. And she is about to tell him something that will impress his superiors. He will be able to help his country.

'Bialla, in the district of Johannisburg, East Prussia.'

'Thought so. Godforsaken place at the end of the world.' He huffs condescendingly, hammering the answer into the keys. It's a scandal that he has to waste his time with women like this. What is she going to complain about? A dirty staircase?

'Matter!'

Agatha says, 'Albert Lange, Schuhstrasse 34, second floor, left door, listens to enemy radio. Each evening. Albert Lange is a healthy, strong man and unfortunately has so far escaped the attention of our Wehrmacht.'

The man stops typing, pulls out his handkerchief once more, unfolds it slowly, holds it in front of this mouth and nose, and clears his throat. His eyes above the handkerchief glance at Agatha. He's misjudged the woman. He nods, removes the handkerchief and stuffs it back into his trouser pocket, this time without folding it first.

'And what's your relationship to this man?'

'He's my son-in-law.'

He likes the comforting feeling of the tongue against the inside of his cheek. Raw skin against raw skin. The black letters once again begin to riddle the paper.

The woman bends down to pick up her bag. He grabs the edge of the desk and lifts himself up. The pain in his stump is severe this morning. Rain must be coming. Nevertheless, he manages to put enough pressure on his wooden leg to walk around the table. He's sorry he underestimated her. His own physical discomfort should not lead him to behave badly.

'Heil Hitler,' he salutes her.

Agatha hesitates. His tongue is moving hectically up and down against the inside of his cheek.

'Heil Hitler,' she mumbles. She does not want to aggravate him unnecessarily.

Trude wears a dark blue suit and a little matching hat. She has powdered her nose, her lips shine red. She smells of expensive perfume.

As she takes off her gloves and pulls the pin out of her hat in front of the mirror in the corridor, she says, 'Albert will fetch me at one o'clock. And I told Peter to come to yours straight after school. I also left a note on our door in case he forgets.'

She unbuttons her suit jacket and hangs it on the hall stand. Underneath it she wears a mother-of-pearl silk blouse.

'Is that new?' Agatha immediately enquires.

'Yes.' Trude spins around in a circle, pulling in her stomach. She is proud of her wasp waist. 'Albert gave it to me as a gift. From Paris.' She brings her face close to the mirror, wets two fingertips and twists a little curl of hair onto her forehead.

'How did he manage to get his hands on a blouse from Paris?' Agatha asks, observing her daughter closely.

Trude shrugs.

'You know, he's got connections.'

She takes a step back from the mirror, places her hands on her hips and looks at herself, pleased.

'You both seem to be getting on again.' Agatha won't let the subject drop.

'Mmm.' Trude smiles at her mirror image.

For a moment Agatha keeps quiet, then she says, 'And what about a couple of months ago? Have you already forgotten?'

Once again, Trude sat in Agatha's sewing room crying her eyes out. Albert had started a new affair. It wasn't the first time.

'Trude, darling, I love only you. But this woman is important to us. With her support I won't be drafted. You wouldn't want that, would you? We both know, this is not our war. We don't want it,' Albert had said.

To him, his explanation and excuse for the affair sounded plausible. And it is indeed true: he loves only Trude. But that doesn't mean he will turn down the offer of a bit of fun on the side when the opportunity arises. Especially if it helps him to avoid the war. As long as the wife of the Gauleiter is well disposed towards him, she will put in a good word with her husband. As an added bonus, she understands his desires. Sometimes Trude can be a bit prudish, especially when she is in a bad mood.

Trude turns to her mother and puts her hands on Agatha's thin shoulders. Her mother always frets about everything, and she doesn't trust Albert. Trude plants a brief kiss on her mother's forehead.

'Don't worry about me.' She turns and heads into the sewing room. 'So where are those dresses?'

Agatha and Trude start work on the dresses. The clatter of the sewing machine alternates with the noise that travels up from the street: the rattle of wheels over cobbles, individual words and fragments of sentences that have lost all meaning. The church bells begin to ring. Three times. For an instant Trude holds her breath, waiting to see if they will sound a fourth time to indicate the full hour, but they don't. Once again, she bows her head over the machine, and her hand with the beautiful sparkling ring descends on to the wheel at the side, giving it a shove, while her foot pushes the pedal. Agatha is stooped over the big wooden table, holding pins between her lips, while her fingers dart nimbly over the fabric that is laid flat on the table.

'Done!' Trude lifts her hand off the wheel. She shifts back in her chair, removes the dress from the sewing machine and shakes it out. She hands it to Agatha. The church bells ring four times, followed by a little break, and then another single ring with a deeper bell. Exactly one o'clock. Trude stands up, stretching herself, then walks out of the room. Agatha hangs the dress on a wall hook and starts to clear the table of fabric scraps, reels of thread and needles. When Trude returns, she has put on her hat and jacket, reapplied colour to her lips and put fresh powder on her nose. She carries her handbag under her arm. She approaches the window and pushes it open wide; the bells ring quarter past.

'I wonder where Albert is.' She leans forward as far as

possible, looking up and down the street. 'The Clausens have invited us for lunch, and they are important to him.' She turns away from the window.

Agatha rolls thread on to the reel with an impassive face.

Trude walks up to her mother and plants a fleeting kiss on her cheek.

The front door slams shut. Agatha hears Trude's high heels clatter down the stairs. She has finished winding the thread and places the reel on the table. Through the open window she watches her daughter rush along the pavement. She turns back to the room and looks at the two dresses hanging on the wall. She steps closer and strokes them with a flat hand. She takes the hem of the yellow one between her fingers and pulls it straight.

Albert's Fate

TRUDE HURRIES ALONG the road. She has a bad feeling in her stomach. Of course, she has waited for Albert many times before, but when they are getting on well, as now, he is always punctual, behaving like a true gentleman.

She turns the corner. A military vehicle is parked outside their house, in front of the entrance to their courtyard. On the other side onlookers have gathered, waiting to see whom they have caught this time. Trude starts running. The Gauleiter slut! She's denounced him. Trude will kill her, scratch out her eyes. At the open gate she collides with men in uniform. They are holding Albert on either side. He is handcuffed. He is wearing his best suit, the grey pinstripe in which he looks so handsome. Trude's brain logs these facts, one after the other. Then she stares into the bewildered face of her husband.

'Albert!'

Her glance jumps from one uniformed man to the next, searching for something in their eyes. Pity, empathy, understanding – a human reaction that would allow her to plead for her husband. But nothing shows in their faces. They try to move past her. Trude stands her ground.

'Where are you taking him?'

Once again her eyes flick from face to face, eventually stopping at Albert's.

'Where are they taking you? Please say something.'

'Make way!' One of the mouths has issued the order.

Trude grabs an arm in a brown shirt, clings to it.

'Please. Tell me where you are taking him.'

The arm shakes, pulling itself free in a single, sweeping motion. Another arm pushes her aside. She trips, manages to stop herself just in time from falling to the cobblestones. From the corner of her eye she notices the black boots moving, thumping the ground hard.

'I told no one.'

Albert looks back over his shoulder while the men drag him along. They shove him into the car. His head flies back and hits the headrest. The car moves on.

Trude feels dizzy. A car hoots its horn.

She sees herself stepping aside slowly, walking through the gate, picking up her handbag from the ground. Deliberate, precise movements. She climbs the stairs to their apartment.

The door stands wide open. She removes the pin from the note that she left for Peter and crumples the piece of paper in her hand. She pushes it into her handbag as she steps inside the apartment. She observes herself casting a glance into the kitchen, the sitting room. Furniture knocked over, drawers torn out of chests, kitchen cabinets emptied on to the floor. She nods to herself as if taking note. They love this kind of work. And the guards downstairs were young lads, seventeen-year-olds, maybe eighteen. They have something to prove, to show how thoroughly they can do their job.

She locks the front door. In front of the mirror in the corridor she takes off her hat. She places it on the small dresser under the mirror next to her handbag. She stands still. She takes in the sight of handbag and hat. Italian-make. She bought both in '38 in Rome. They are stylish items that will never go out of fashion. Trude strokes the handbag. She adores the way these two elegant accessories lie next to each other. On a small dresser in the corridor. Signalling the presence of a woman with status. Who runs the most successful photographic studio in town.

Whose husband will now be sent to war.

In the sitting room she picks up a chair from the floor and sits at the table. Shouldn't she cry? Rage? Instead her body feels as if it is a separate entity from her. A very still, heavy container among all the destruction around her: the glass cabinet smashed, the curtain rail hanging loose, books pulled from the case and scattered across the floor.

She straightens the tablecloth, strokes it with the flat of her hand. Surely Albert will walk back at any moment. That's his style. With a mischievous glint in his eyes, a cigarette at the corner of his mouth and his hat slightly tilted to one side. Trude can already feel her body jumping up from the chair and running towards him, taking the cigarette out of his mouth and kissing him. And he laughs and says, 'That was a close call.' And they make love.

She should tidy up before he comes home.

On the threshold of the bedroom she stops with a start, as if she has remembered something. A vague inkling she had earlier. Suddenly she wants to turn back, knows she shouldn't go in here, even look. But too late.

The devastation in the bedroom is greater than anywhere else. All the clothes and the bed linen have been pulled out of the wardrobe and scattered across the room. Some torn to shreds. The mattress slashed from top to bottom, the duvet too. Feathers everywhere – as if some animal has been ripped to pieces. Trude holds on to the door frame; she notices her shaking hand as her eyes scan the room. Her mind knows what she's looking for but refuses to name it. It's not among the scattered things, so there is a chance they didn't find it. For a fleeting moment she hopes against hope, against all reason. Because if they came to search for the radio, someone must have informed on them. Maybe she misunderstood Albert, that's not what he meant when he said, 'I told no one.' He's no fool. He would never put Peter and her at risk, just so he could boast about listening to the enemy.

The only other person who could have known about it is Peter. And if Peter knew, her mother knew too.

Trude's hand is now shaking so badly that she wants to remove it from the door frame, but she can't. She has lost control over it. She grasps her shaking left hand with her right and brings them both together in front of her. Pressing them into her stomach stops the shaking.

Peter sneaks through the apartment in the evenings when he's supposed to be in bed, and he loves trading secrets with his grandmother. Trude knows her mother. She'd do anything to protect her daughter and grandson.

And listening to the enemy radio is one of the most dangerous things.

Trude steps forward, facing the wardrobe. It's empty. Totally empty. They found what they came for and that's why they took Albert.

No. No. No. Peter wouldn't have told his grandmother. Why should he? Listening to the radio is nothing special. They all listen to the radio together at the weekend. And so hearing his parents listen to it in the evenings wouldn't have seemed strange or anything special that he needed to tell his grandmother. No, Peter didn't tell Agatha. And Agatha wouldn't have gone to the police. She doesn't like Albert, still thinks he is vulgar and from the gutter. She doesn't understand what Albert makes Trude feel like when he swings her around as they dance, when Trude knows that she is the best dancer Albert has ever held in his arms. But Agatha would never have put Albert's head on the block. And snitching on him to the police means signing his death warrant. Agatha understands this as much as anyone else. They will send him to war. And Albert is no soldier.

No, her mother is not an evil person. The police came on spec. They don't need firm evidence. All they require is a vague tip-off, a nebulous reason to kick into action, to flex their ridiculous muscles. To turn a place upside down. And by chance they got lucky this time. It has happened to others, and this time it was their turn.

Trude removes her jacket, picks up a hanger that has been kicked under the bed and hangs the jacket in the wardrobe.

Albert will talk his way out of the situation. He's got contacts everywhere. Done a lot of people favours. They owe him.

She starts tidying, returning dresses, skirts, blouses, suits, jackets to their proper places. The torn stuff she sets to one side. Most of it isn't actually damaged that badly. She and her mother will be able to mend the pieces in a couple of evenings.

Closing the once again neat and tidy wardrobe, Trude feels better. She's done good work.

After examining the slashed mattress – this is beyond repair, they'll have to get a new one – she turns her attention to her dressing table. Boxes of powder tipped over, perfume bottles emptied. She puts a couple of unbroken flacons on the windowsill, then fetches the metal bin from the kitchen and sweeps the broken mess into it with one broad movement of her lower arm. Too late she remembers that she runs the risk of cutting herself. Splinters enter her flesh. Holding her breath, she sits down on the bed and pulls out the pieces of glass one by one. There is no time to linger over the pain; she has things to do. The place has to be returned to normality. Albert will be back soon. The least she can do is spare him the sight of a ransacked home. She grabs an old scarf that she didn't put back in the wardrobe and wipes the top of her dressing table until no marks remain.

In the kitchen most of the crockery and kitchenware has been smashed. Trude is now working fast. Within ten minutes she has scooped the broken pieces into two baskets that she will take downstairs later.

She sighs. She should look after herself so that she doesn't appear too frazzled when Albert walks back in. After all, he will have experienced a far greater fright than she. They might even have mistreated him at the police station. Trude wants to be ready to comfort him, to take him in her arms.

She opens the oven door and gropes with the flat of her hand inside the stovepipe until she finds the little packet. They have turned the entire apartment upside down, but they didn't find this! Chuckling, she pulls out the precious packet of real coffee and brews up an extra-strong cup. Then she hides the packet again.

At the table in the sitting room she drinks her coffee with closed eyes, breathing in the wonderful smell. She leans back in the chair, slides off her shoes, stretches her legs, puts one foot on top of the other and lifts them a few centimetres off the ground. Gently she lets them bob up and down. She holds the cup with both hands. She drinks slowly. As long as she is waiting – and no one disturbs her wait – Albert will return.

That's what has always happened when Trude has been waiting for Albert.

Peter is whistling, running up the stairs to his apartment two steps at a time – to strengthen his leg muscles. It's his new regime: running up the stairs two at a time, no more dawdling about; he has to get fit and build his strength for the Stargard Boxing World Championships. School finished at midday and so he and Johann Windrose have been training for the finals for the last couple of hours. The Stargard Boxing World Championships don't, of course, exist yet, but Peter and Johann will set them up. Soon. At break today, Peter told his friend that he had enough money to get one pair of gloves at least, maybe two. Johann was very impressed.

'If *you* get the gloves, I will let you win,' he suggested.

'No way.' Peter shook his head. 'A boxing match has to be fair. The better boxer will win.'

After school they went to Herr Friedrichs and asked him if he would mind writing a letter to his son, the war hero and boxing champion, with a request to act as referee during the forthcoming Stargard Boxing World Championships. They, that is Peter and Johann, would of course hold back on any further organization until Herr Friedrichs's son returned from the front. Herr Friedrichs was very moved and replied with tears in his eyes that he would be honoured to write the letter; and his son would undoubtedly be delighted to accept the invitation. Heil Hitler.

The first thing Peter will do in a moment is count is money. He thinks it's sixty marks, but maybe it's even more. He should do one more note exchange, perhaps tonight. No, tonight is too soon. He shakes his head, slightly out of breath. It's always best to let a few weeks elapse between exchange trips.

One more flight of stairs. Come on, boy, push. In his inner ear he hears Herr Friedrichs blow his whistle, the one he uses during sports lessons. Three more steps. Peter takes them in one go. Lands on both feet at the top, then nearly falls back, his hand tightening around the banister. Yes! He's a hero. He pulls the other arm up in victory, then he wipes the sweat from his forehead and rings the doorbell.

No sound. No movement.

'Mum!'

She didn't tell him to go to Omi's today, so she should be in. He begins to step from one foot to the other. He really needs a pee.

'Mum!'

He kicks against the door. Nothing. OK, he's got no choice but to sprint back down and to the yard. He drops his satchel and has already placed his hands on the banister when he hears the door opening.

As Peter pulls up his shorts and holds his hands under the water – he glances at the bar of soap but decides he can do that later – he senses something strange in the air.

'Peter, come here. We need to talk.'

His mother is closing the door, with his satchel in her hand. She looks strange. Really pale.

'I'm sorry I'm late. Johann and I—'

That's what it is. He can't smell cooking. That's what's so strange. His tummy immediately begins to rumble. He's reached his mother. She takes him by the shoulders and gently

48

pushes him into the sitting room towards the sofa. The room is a mess.

'Why—'

He looks around. His mother has sat down next to him.

'Peter, listen. The police—'

She interrupts herself. No, she shouldn't mention that they came to take Albert away. She should have thought beforehand what to say to her son. How would it feel for a boy to think his father has been taken away – in handcuffs? Boys want their fathers to be heroes. For Peter's – and Albert's – sake, she shouldn't tell her son the truth.

Peter isn't aware that his mother has stopped talking. All he heard was the word 'police' and everything inside him went flat. Dead. The police want to arrest him. He's a thief. He's always known it. It's not an exchange business. He steals money. And now the police have found out. Somehow. And his mother knows too.

'Mum.'

His lower lip starts to quiver. He's not a thief. He needs to explain. He's so sorry. He doesn't want to go to prison. Dear God, no.

'I—' he begins.

'*Shh.*' Trude's eyes are now tear-filled too. She pulls her son into her arms. 'Dad will come back.' She strokes his hair. 'As a war hero. Many fathers fight in the war.' She rocks her son back and forth, and buries her nose in his hair.

War hero? His dad? Peter is turning his head to the side, gasping for air. His mother is pressing him too hard against her chest.

'I can't breathe.'

Trude loosens her embrace.

His dad doesn't like fighting. He doesn't like the war either. Peter doesn't understand.

'But you said the police were coming,' he whispers. He avoids saying 'police' too loudly in case they are already standing outside the door and can hear them talking.

For a few moments more his mother continues to rock him silently. Then she says, 'When you rang the doorbell I thought it was the police because someone broke into our flat . . . after Dad had gone.'

'Don't let the police in.' Peter frees himself from his mother. 'Please.'

Tears are now rolling down his cheeks. The police smell a thief when they see one. And even though they are not coming here looking for him, they will realize that he's a thief and arrest him. There and then. On the spot.

'I don't like the police,' he says, weeping.

It breaks Trude's heart to see Peter like this. He's only a little boy. Seeing him in such distress proves he's aware that he might have done something that he shouldn't have. That he told his grandmother about the secret radio. He wouldn't have told any of the boys. That's not what they talk about. Peter didn't know what he was doing.

Trude feels dizzy again.

They should have been more careful. Now they have implicated Peter, their own son, with their reckless behaviour. As a child, he shouldn't feel such agony.

'Come here.' Trude pulls Peter towards her again. 'I won't let the police in, do you hear me?'

Peter nods and she wraps her arms around him. If she could she would take him back inside her, to protect him from all the pain and all the evil. For ever.

'There is only one thing you have to promise me: that you will never mention to anyone . . . that you knew about the radio . . . the radio in the wardrobe . . . and that you told Oma. Will you promise me?'

'I promise,' Peter mumbles against his mother's chest. Although truth to tell, he's not sure why his mother is bringing up the radio. But anyway, that's an easy thing to promise.

He's still sobbing. More from shock, though. This time he got away. But next time? Maybe the thieves took his piggy bank? Peter suddenly hopes so. Then all the evidence will be gone. And if they didn't take it, he will need to get rid of it – piggy bank and money. Bury it somewhere. Or better still, throw it into the Madüsee. He will ask Johann's big brother to row him out on to the lake where it's deepest. Johann's big brother does anything for money. And if Peter wraps the piggy bank in a piece of cloth, no one will be able to tell what he's throwing into the water. As for the gloves and the boxing world championships – he will tell Johann that thieves stole the money and that they have to find a different way of getting the gloves. And as for his dad going to war, Peter isn't really that upset. So many fathers are fighting in the war. Johann's dad too. And sometimes in fact Peter used to worry that he was the only boy who didn't have a war hero as a dad. Now he no longer needs to worry.

The only thing that bugs Peter a bit is that his grandma clearly didn't keep her promise and told his mum that he knew about the secret radio. So Omi can't keep secrets. He'd better not tell her any more.

On the street Trude doesn't look up, keeps her head low. She clutches her handbag under her arm. She would love to walk with her head held high, proud and with a straight back, but that is impossible. She doesn't want to meet the neighbours' glances and doesn't want them to see her face swollen from crying. She hasn't even put on any lipstick and looks like a common woman with a tear-stained face whose husband or brother or son has just been taken away, has just died. There are thousands and thousands of these women. She feels ashamed to be one of them now. She has always been so proud not to belong to them, to be different, to be clever enough to have tricked everyday life with its wars and politics, to have found a way to ignore it. Now she is one of those normal women. Worse: now she is a woman whose mother has betrayed her own daughter by denouncing her son-in-law. How is that possible?

Trude walks past her mother and straight into the sewing room, feeling the dried tears on her cheeks. She has asked Peter to stay downstairs in the yard and play with the other children until she calls him up for lunch. Agatha hurries into the kitchen, fills a glass of water. She puts it in front of Trude, who has sat down at the big table. Agatha clears away the blouse that she's been cutting and slips it over the dummy. Then she too sits down, at an angle to her daughter.

For a while neither of the women speaks.

'I know it must hurt.'

Trude doesn't react.

'Remember, you're not alone. Many women share the same fate.'

Trude still doesn't react.

'He might return. It's in God's hands now.'

Trude lifts her head abruptly.

'God? God didn't report him!' Her voice has suddenly turned shrill.

You, you reported him, she wants to scream out loud. But then she doesn't want to scream it out loud. No! How can she even consider screaming? Does she want the whole world to know what her mother did? And what if it wasn't her mother after all who betrayed Albert? Just because Peter knew. Trude, how can you accuse your mother, your own mother, of such a crime? Imagine saying it out loud – now. Imagine your mother's face – here right in front of you – turning into a mask of horror and pain. She has always only ever wanted the best for you. She doesn't deserve to be accused of a crime she might not have committed. Couldn't have committed. What has Agatha done to deserve a daughter who is even able to harbour such thoughts about her own mother? Who is the evil one!

And let's face it, even if your mother had gone to the police, she would have done it not to hurt you but to save you. And save Peter. You should have told your mother about the radio from the start, reassuring her that you – you and Albert – are careful, that you know the risks. But you went behind your mother's back. What torment your mother must have gone through when she heard from Peter about the radio! How could you possibly have done that to her? Again, you have no one to blame but yourself for the tragedy that you are now all facing.

These are the thoughts that go through Trude's mind as her glance falls on Agatha's small, hard-working hands that for once are lying still in her lap. And she suddenly remembers how she so desperately wanted to get to her mother in hospital when Agatha was pregnant with her small brother. And how she was prevented from doing so. And she remembers that afterwards she sometimes used to fantasize that if only she had got to the hospital, her mother would have seen her and the sight of her daughter would have made her happy and nothing bad would ever have happened to the baby. And now Trude's brother would have been a man and Agatha's world would have been fine. Instead there is only Trude. And if Trude turns against Agatha, against her own mother, what would be left for Agatha?

Her mother is no angel. And she never liked Albert. But she would never do anything to hurt her daughter. And Trude is now hurting. Very badly.

A violent sob breaks uncontrollably from her. 'Who could have done such an evil thing?'

For a moment Agatha is paralysed by the desperate sound of the cry. Then she pushes her chair closer to Trude's, puts her arms around her daughter and draws her close. She rocks her gently back and forth.

'Shh.'

Trude cries for a long time. Her mother's embrace feels so warm. So utterly familiar. So safe. How can she have contemplated, even for a split second, destroying this sense of belonging?

Finally the sobbing subsides. Trude frees herself and opens her bag, rummaging around for a handkerchief. There are many people, many more than she thought, who probably knew about their Black Radio, or at least guessed that they possessed one. There are so many envious people. That slut must have denounced him. A jealous viper who couldn't bear the fact that Albert returned to Trude, to his wife.

'Let's go into the kitchen.' Agatha stands up. 'Let's get some lunch.'

'I will tackle that woman,' says Trude calmly, standing in the door to the kitchen.

Agatha walks over to the cooker. Instinctively she knows who her daughter is referring to. The woman Albert had an affair with recently.

'I wouldn't do that. You don't want more trouble, especially not with people like that.'

She turns on the gas and lights the flame underneath the pot on the stove.

'But I can't just sit here and do nothing.'

'You have to think of yourself and Peter now.' Agatha stirs the soup in the pot. 'You can go back to Dr Strade. I know that he's looking for a new assistant. I'm sure he would take you on, even though you never finished your apprenticeship. He knows you're honest and hard-working.'

'I'm no longer a secretary. Albert and I own a business that I have been running for the last few years.'

'You won't get any new supplies in now he is gone,' Agatha says matter-of-factly, while skimming the fat off the soup.

Trude crumples her handkerchief in her hands.

'I will try,' she replies, even though she knows her mother is right. 'I will keep the studio going for as long as I can. Until Albert returns.'

Agatha reaches across the table and opens the glass cabinet to take out three bowls. She puts them on the table. With a movement of her head, she says to her daughter, 'Call Peter up. We're having ham soup today. It'll do you good.'

It all happened as Agatha predicted. After a few months Trude had to close the studio and she and Peter moved back in with her mother. Trude returned to work for Dr Strade, who encouraged her to study in the evenings to obtain her high-school qualification.

In her mind, Trude had made peace with the inevitable, clinging to the story that she told everyone: someone had tipped off the police, they had come to their apartment on spec and got lucky. To begin with she observed her mother closely for any sign of remorse or even satisfaction that Albert was gone, but Agatha only ever showed real compassion whenever Trude broke down in tears. She was always ready to listen and soothe her daughter. And Agatha did suffer with Trude. It hurt her to see her daughter in such emotional pain. But Agatha was also convinced that her daughter had been naive in allowing Albert to own a Black Radio. And so Trude had left her mother no choice: Agatha had had to save her daughter and her grandson.

Needless to say, overall Agatha was pleased. Things were finally going in the right direction. And not only for Trude with Dr Strade, but also for Peter, who loved the boxing club his grandmother now took him to twice a week.

And for Christmas 1944, Agatha bought Peter his first pair of boxing gloves. As the boy unwrapped his present under the Christmas tree, Agatha smiled contentedly. She was looking forward to the new year.

PART II: FLIGHT

Heading West

EVERY PART OF the big hall and right along the platforms as far as Trude can see is occupied by bodies. People are lying and sitting and standing. Suitcases and rucksacks, duvets and blankets, pots and pans strapped together with string. Wooden boxes with chickens, and children. The stench of urine and wet clothes. The filth, the dirt, the unhygienic conditions – it's overwhelming. She breathes as shallowly as possible. Her eyes search the hall but can't make out anyone official-looking. Slowly she starts moving to the right where, at the far end, the ticket office is situated. She tries to make her way between the bodies, but it's not easy. She steps on legs, on arms, even nearly on a child. For a couple of moments she stands still, wondering if she should turn back. But back is now no longer an option. The ticket office is less than a hundred metres away. She has to reach it. She shuffles forward, pushing her feet along the floor in the hope of encouraging bodies to move slightly to the left or the right.

The stench comes from below, then rises up above the bodies and above Trude's head, where it transforms into an invisible membrane trapping beneath it air drained of oxygen and instead filled with unbreathable lethargy, exhaustion – and silent fear. This many living bodies should create a wriggling, buzzing, noisy group. But they have metamorphosed into a comatose muddy mass through which Trude is wading. She clenches her arms so close to her stomach that it hurts. Her body won't ever be pulled down into that morass. Her body will never lie there, having lost all contours, all individuality, being trodden on and shoved about.

She keeps her eyes firmly fixed on the windows of the ticket office. She can now see all of them, even the ones that were initially hidden by a big pillar. The black blinds seem to be drawn. She squints. The bad air burns her eyes. They are watering and the tears blur her vision. Still, she won't lose hope. No. It's impossible they are closed. It's late morning on a Thursday. Banks, train stations, shops, doctors' surgeries – everyone has to open on a Thursday! Maybe the ticket sellers have gone for an early lunch? Well, once she has reached the windows, there will surely be signs to inform her when they will open again so she can buy their tickets.

Against her stomach Trude feels the money belt that her mother made last night by using part of the old corset from the dummy and some leftover brocade curtain material. The two women sat side by side at the big table, working fast and silently. While Agatha made the belt, Trude opened up the lining of her mother's winter coat. Then she sewed into the inside her diamond ring, her ruby brooch and her pearl necklace, putting a double cross-stitch after each pearl. Initially they wondered if they should sew the jewellery into the front or the back of the coat. Eventually they decided on the front, so Agatha would be able to lie on her back with her coat on. Just in case they have to sleep in unheated hotels.

Trude has reached the ticket office. An inaudible sigh of relief escapes her. Now she will find out when the next train to Berlin leaves. They need to get to Berlin. That's how she and Albert lived during their years of travel: they found a place in a big city where work and accommodation were easily available.

The ticket office windows stare at Trude with their blank, dead eyes. There are too many blank dead eyes staring at her in this awful city. Inside this train station. Outside, where there are holes that once used to be windows. That is, if the walls of the bombed-out houses are still standing. Many buildings have collapsed and are now just heaps of rubble.

It was her mother's idea to leave. Agatha started talking about it weeks ago. East Prussian refugees had begun to pass through the town in ever bigger numbers, heading west. Poor, sick, emaciated creatures who often carried all their possessions in bundles on their backs.

'Trude, we have to leave. The front is approaching. Our town, too, will be evacuated soon. And then everyone will be on the move. If we leave now, we'll have a head start. We'll get somewhere safe, find a place to stay and wait till we can return. We have enough money to last us some weeks.'

Trude shook her head. 'I can't leave. What if Albert returns and doesn't find us here? And anyway, the fighting won't ever reach us. It hasn't done so for the last five years.'

But when an SS battalion arrived and rumours spread that they were hiding and an Allied bombing attack was imminent and civilians would be evacuated any day soon, Trude agreed to leave. She wrote a note for Albert, just in case he returned when they had gone. She hadn't heard from him in months. But as she knew from other women, no news was good news. Or, at least, hope for good news. If he'd been killed she'd have been notified. 'Dear Albert, please don't worry about us. We will be back in a few days, a couple of weeks at the most. In the cold room there are a few jars of bottled vegetables and fruit. Trude.' In the meantime, Agatha wiped quickly over the sideboard in the sitting room and the two dark yellow lampshades where the dust always settled. Then she walked one last time through the apartment to make sure that the electrics were turned off. They locked the front door and Trude went up on tiptoes to hide the key on the ledge above the door. Albert would expect to find it there if no one opened the door when he rang the bell. Under the cover of night, they travelled on the back of a lorry to Stettin. Agatha paid well for that trip.

But what if Berlin looks the same? Destroyed? Reduced to rubble? Trude shakes her head. Berlin is too big. There might be areas that look like this, but not everywhere. That's impossible.

'Can I help you?' A ticket inspector has materialized out of thin air. He wears a uniform and his hat. There is some order here after all! Or are her weak nerves now playing tricks? For a split second Trude is tempted to stretch out her hand to touch the man to see if he is real. Then she manages to smile – more to herself than to him.

'We are trying to get to Berlin today. Could you please tell me when the next train leaves and where I can buy tickets?'

'There are no trains today.' He makes a sweeping gesture with his hand as if that explains the 'no trains'.

'Oh!' Trude is confused. There must be trains. 'Will there be trains tomorrow?'

'Yes, tomorrow.' Again the ticket inspector makes the same gesture.

Trude notices that his hand is shaking. It doesn't sound as if he knows much. Still, he's her best bet.

'What time is the first train, sir?' she continues.

'Come early, madam. As early as possible.' He lifts his cap and walks away. Just as he is about to disappear out of sight, he stops, seeming to have thought of something else: 'The trains are no longer running according to schedule.' Then he walks away.

Once again Trude stares at the blank ticket-office windows. And they stare back at her. Blankly.

She notices a glass case to the right containing what looks like the train times. On the floor in front of it sits an old couple with their backs against the wall and their eyes closed. Trude steps over their legs and studies the timetable. Prenzlau 05:35 is the first train. She decides then and there that that's their train and they will change in Prenzlau for Berlin. As long as they get out of this town as quickly as possible and are heading west, they should be safe.

'There are no trains today. There might be some tomorrow.'

Trude lowers her gaze. The old woman has opened her pus-filled eyes. Her husband's head has sunk on to her shoulder. His mouth is wide open. The woman pulls out her hand from underneath her cloak. It is covered in bright red, bleeding scabies bites. Instinctively – and in shock and disgust – Trude takes a step back.

'Please, *junge Frau*, can you spare some money or something to eat?'

For a moment Trude can't tear her glance away from the hand that is stretching out towards her. She doesn't want to be touched by it at any cost. When she eventually makes her way back to the entrance through the mass of bodies, she feels ashamed. But if these people have scabies, they will also be infested with fleas and lice. No wonder no one wants to give them anything – not food, or work, or a bed. They – she, Agatha and Peter – will never sink that low. How could they? Trude knows a couple of good, inexpensive hotels in Berlin. They are not poor farm labourers from the sticks. Agatha is a well-known, respected seamstress, and for years Trude ran the most famous photographic studio in town. They know how to behave, how to dress, how to talk the talk. And during her travels with Albert, Trude acquired a cosmopolitan chic that works wonders when she turns on the charm. It shouldn't be too difficult for either her or Agatha to find some temporary work if they need to stay away a bit longer. The war will surely be over very soon now. They have packed enough proof that they are respectable, trustworthy, hard-working people: Trude's school-leaving certificate, old invoices from Trude and Albert's studio, a couple of payslips from Dr Strade, thank-you notes from Agatha's satisfied clients. And also a few photographs of dresses that Agatha made, of Peter's first day at school.

Trude stumbles outside and the cold air hits. It has started to snow again. She turns her face to the sky. To feel the snowflakes melt on her flushed skin is a beautiful sensation.

'When is our train?'

Peter is pulling on his mother's coat. Agatha is standing with the two suitcases beneath a balcony projecting from the station building, trying to shelter from the snow.

'There are no trains today.' Trude walks towards her mother. 'We should try to find a room for the night here.' They exchange a brief glance, and Agatha notices how blood-shot Trude's eyes are.

'Let's go and find a café first,' Agatha says, bending down to pick up both suitcases. 'Peter can have hot chocolate and we can get warm.'

'We shouldn't waste our money in cafés.'

Maybe Trude should have listened to her mother after all and they should have left last week. She takes the brown suitcase out of Agatha's hand. 'Albert and I bought them in Paris,' she'd commented last night as she fetched them down from the top of the big wardrobe. 'How lucky that we have them. Otherwise we would have to bundle everything up like the poor devils from the East.'

'We will only have a hot drink.' Agatha has started to walk towards the road. 'And eat our sandwiches in the hotel later.' She takes Peter's hand and squeezes it conspiratorially. 'How about some cream on top of your chocolate?'

They are waiting to be seated. It's pleasantly uncrowded. A few elderly gentlemen drinking their late-morning coffee while reading the papers and a couple of ladies in hats and fashionable dresses sipping tea, eating cake and gossiping. Chandeliers hang from the high ceiling. Along the walls there are big mirrors. Trude makes a mental note to come back here on a day trip with Albert once they've returned home, to drink mocha and indulge in a cognac or two. She quickly pulls off her woollen hat, aware that it isn't really suitable for this sort of place. With a raised eyebrow she orders Peter to do the same. The concierge vanished behind a curtain the moment they stepped inside the café. A couple of waiters hurry busily past them. Agatha has already spotted the perfect table for them. Right next to the large, tiled stove. Peter might be able to secretly take off his boots underneath the table. Agatha notices her grandson's longing glances in the direction of the cream cakes behind the glass counter. They might share a piece after all.

The concierge reappears, followed by the head waiter, who takes in the suitcase standing next to Agatha with a dismissive glance.

'What can I do for you?' the concierge asks in a surprisingly sharp tone, without any greeting, indication of a bow or even the slightest hint of a nod.

At first Agatha is taken aback. 'I . . . we . . .' she stutters. Then she gets hold of herself. 'We would like a table for three.'

The concierge runs his eyes up and down her body with outrageous impertinence. Eventually they remain fixed on her suitcase before they jump to her face. 'We don't serve refugees here.' Before Agatha has time to reply, he walks past her and opens the door. 'May I ask you to leave.'

Trude has already picked up the other suitcase and started to turn towards the door. Peter is staring at Agatha, who feels her chin trembling. Out of anger or despair or insult or hurt, she doesn't know. All she knows is that they are not refugees and she won't be treated this way.

'Sir,' she starts.

But Trude interrupts her. 'Mum, please let's go.'

'Omi, please.'

Peter tugs at his grandmother's sleeve as she edges a little closer to the headwaiter. Her anger has suddenly evaporated, her chin has stopped trembling. These two men are misjudging the facts, misguided by their own fear and by orders from above. Agatha will correct them and, while she's at it, she might as well tell a little story to amuse Peter.

'Sir, I must apologize.' She smiles at the headwaiter sweetly, though he is as ugly as sin, with a big wart on his chin. 'How silly of us to walk in here with suitcases. In these times.'

She rolls her eyes and simultaneously tries to pretend that Trude isn't there. She feels her daughter's incredulous stare on her back.

'Let me introduce myself.' She takes off her mitten and stretches out her hand to the headwaiter. 'I'm Agatha Weiss. And this is my daughter, Trude Lange, the famous actress, and her son. They have just arrived with their chaffeur from Berlin in order for us to spend a couple of hours together. Afterwards my daughter will travel further east to pay tribute to our boys at the front.'

Agatha continues smiling at the headwaiter. She is now wearing an elegant tailored grey suit. Her hair is pinned up exquisitely, a delicate hat balancing on the top. She lowers her gaze and turns her hand slowly so that he may bend down and bow over it. For a fleeting moment she hopes he has manners enough not to place a wet kiss on the back of her hand. Only philistines would behave in such a way.

The headwaiter appears to be paralysed. Agatha continues to look at her hand with the sort of demeanour that befits the mother of a famous actress. Or singer. Yes, a singer. Like Zara Leander. A demeanour that calls for conciliatory action on the part of the headwaiter but also hints at her willingness to forgive his faux pas. After all, they live in difficult times. Oh, please let this work. She feels the heat rising. The headwaiter still hasn't made his move. She's about to draw her arm back with an air of outraged indignation when she notices his gloved hand. Briefly, it touches hers gently, while he bows without placing his lips on her skin. The perfect gentleman. This time her smile is real. She nods in recognition of his action and as a sign of her pardon. He straightens and she lets him pick up both suitcases as the three of them follow him to their chosen table. He brings the menu cards.

'I hope, *gnädige Frau*, you will accept our invitation to lunch on the house.'

As soon as the headwaiter has left, Peter breaks out in giggles. Trude kicks her son fiercely under the table and flashes him warning glances.

'But Omi lied,' Peter says, looking at his mother with a hurt expression.

'She didn't lie. We're not refugees, are we?'

He shakes his head.

'There you go. Grandma exaggerated a bit, that's all. Now let's not talk about this any further, otherwise we might not get our lunch.'

Agatha hasn't said a word. She's smiling contentedly.

After the meal Peter falls asleep with his head in her lap. Her expression turns gentle as she strokes his hair.

'He's exhausted, the poor boy,' Agatha explains to the headwaiter. 'He gets carsick. The chauffeur is having the car cleaned at the moment.'

'There is absolutely no rush, *gnädige Frau*. You can see we are not very busy today and it's a pleasure to have such famous guests among us.' He bows again.

They turn into a small side road. The receptionist in the last hotel said they should try here.

Agatha stops dead in her tracks. 'I'm not going there with the boy.'

'What do you suggest we do?' Trude's voice is harsh, her eyes glimmer acrimoniously at her mother. It feels as if they've been to every hotel and guest house in town. Everywhere is full – or so they've been told each time, as they've been turned away again and again.

'Do your actress thing again,' Peter has begged his grandmother a few times.

Each time Agatha has shaken her head. 'It won't work, Peter.'

Instead Trude told them more or less the truth. That they are heading to Berlin. And why not? They have nothing to hide. The replies have always been the same: 'No room available, madam. I'm sorry, madam.' She has also offered more money. 'I'm sorry, we are fully booked.' And they have been pointed to ever smaller, ever sleazier places.

'This looks like a brothel to me. We can't take the boy there,' Agatha snaps at her daughter.

'What's a brothel?' Peter asks. His feet are so frozen, it hurts if he tries to move his toes.

'*Pfui*, don't use that word.' Agatha grabs Peter's jaw between the fingers of her right hand and squeezes it tight. 'It's a dirty word and I will wash out your mouth with soap.'

'Mum, stop it. You've just used that word yourself!'

Agatha lets go of Peter, glaring at Trude.

At this moment Peter doesn't like either his mother or his grandmother. The trip was a bad idea from the very beginning. And they know it. When his mother woke him last night and said they were going on an adventure, travelling on trains and sleeping in hotels, he immediately sensed something fishy. 'But I have school in the morning,' he protested. A look of utter confusion had flickered across his mother's face. Then she muttered, 'I've talked to Herr Friedrichs. It's fine. We'll be back next week.' She bent forward and gave him a kiss on the forehead.

'Why are we still out on the street? Where is my bed?' At least the tears feel warm on his cheeks.

'Mum, please let me ask. This is our last chance.' Appeasingly, Trude places her hand on her mother's arm.

For a moment the two women look at each other above the boy's head. Then Agatha takes Peter's hand and strides past her daughter in the direction of the heart sign that in better times probably flashed all night. Trude, carrying both suitcases, struggles to keep up with them.

'I will go in,' Agatha says at the entrance. 'Peter, hold on to your mother.'

A couple of minutes later she returns. 'They have room with a double bed. It's by the hour. We have it till five in the morning.'

Trude supervises Peter's tooth-brushing while Agatha inspects the mattress for bedbugs then turns it around. To think of the people who have slept on this mattress and what might have happened on it. *Igitt. Igitt. Igitt.* A shiver of disgust runs down Agatha's spine right into her little toe. The idea of hotels and sleeping in beds that hundreds of people have slept in before is disgusting at the best of times, but this is a million times worse. She goes down on her knees in front of the bed, folds her hands, closes her eyes and says the Lord's Prayer. It can't do any harm. When she opens her eyes again, Peter and Trude have already lain down. Fully dressed in their coats. It's too cold in the room to undress. Agatha climbs into the bed. They huddle close. The boy lies between them. Soon Trude and Peter fall asleep. Agatha can't. She doesn't want them to miss the train. They have to get out of this awful town. Perhaps leaving home was a bad idea.

She shakes her head. She cannot get up. She leans with her back against the wall. Trude is standing in front of her.

'We have to go. We have to get on that train.'

Agatha watches her daughter's mouth moving but can't hear her. Peter has nestled up close to his grandmother. He is stroking her head. Agatha feels so sorry that the boy has to stroke her head. But she can't help it.

Trude is kneeling down.

'We have to catch this train, Mum.'

Agatha nods.

'Omi!' Peter wants to go home. Really badly. He doesn't want any more adventures.

And his grandma clearly doesn't want any more either.

'Everything is fine. Shh, everything is fine. And I will be fine too,' she soothes herself and her grandson at the same time.

The masses have set themselves in motion behind Trude's back, heading towards the train, the last one for today. All day they've tried to board a train. But each time the wagons were packed before they could get on. Cattle trucks. They are packing them now into cattle trucks. Like animals.

'We were right to leave. Do you hear me? You were right, Mum. They are evacuating the towns east of here. Do you hear me? That's why everyone here is so desperate to leave. Tomorrow this place will be flooded with even more fleeing people.'

Agatha shakes her head. She doesn't want to hear. 'We are not fleeing,' she whispers. 'We are not fleeing.'

71

Crouching closer to her mother, Trude puts her arms around Agatha's neck and leans her forehead against her mother's face.

'We have a little advantage,' she whispers. 'These aren't the masses yet. The masses will arrive tomorrow, the day after. They won't be able to put on enough trains. And who knows, they might stop them altogether. We have no choice. We have to go.'

Agatha's eyes are closed. She feels the weight of Trude's forehead on hers, hears her breathing. That's what's important. To be close to Trude. To her daughter. To feel her breath, to feel her weight. Agatha adjusts her breathing to match Trude's. She could remain like this for ever.

'We have to go,' she eventually hears Trude say again.

Agatha opens her eyes and nods.

They are squeezing into the crowd that is moving towards the platform. Trude is carrying both suitcases while Agatha is holding Peter's hand. Agatha tastes the stench on her tongue, is aware of the fleas and lice and mites, the pus and other unhealthy fluids being excreted by the bodies around them. She glances down at Peter. Only his hands and face aren't covered.

'Put on your hat and gloves,' she hisses.

She wants to stop but can't. The crowd is pushing them forward. Trude is walking right in front of them. The woman next to Agatha is carrying a chicken crate that is pushing against Agatha's leg. The smell from the crate is ferocious; Agatha gasps for air in order not to retch.

Peter tries to pull his right hand out of Agatha's. She tightens her grip.

'I can't put on my gloves if you hold my hand,' he points out matter-of-factly.

'We're coming to a barrier,' Trude says from the front. 'I think they're taking away the animal crates.' After a couple of moments she adds, 'They're taking away all the luggage.'

Someone steps on Agatha's heel from behind. She looks over her shoulder and into the face of a drooling girl. The woman next to her mumbles, 'I'm so sorry, madam, I'm so sorry.'

No. They can't take everything away from them. Agatha won't let that happen. She stretches out her free hand towards the handle of the brown suitcase that Trude is carrying.

'Give it to me.' She pulls it towards her with such force that Trude has to let go. The suitcase bumps against the chicken crate and the bird begins to make a racket. Agatha ignores the noise and lifts the suitcase to her chest, letting go of Peter's hand.

'Hold your mother's coat with both hands,' she orders Peter, already opening the suitcase in front of her chest. She pushes her hand and arm inside, feeling in the side pocket for the cardboard folder with the certificates, letters and photos. Suddenly she notices that Peter is no longer next to her.

'Peter?' she screams in a high-pitched voice, and lets go of the cardboard folder. In slow motion she notices Trude's shocked face turning back towards her. For a fleeting second Agatha stops moving. A gap between her and Trude appears. The suitcase opens wide and everything falls out.

'Mum!'

Trude turns her head to the left and spots Peter, who has been pushed off to the side. People are squeezing past him and he's falling further and further behind. Dropping the other suitcase, Trude braces her body against the wave of people. Peter is stretching out his arms towards his mother and she manages to grab his hand, pulling him towards her. She scoops him up and pushes forcefully forward to catch up with Agatha, hugging her son to her chest as she glimpses the mother-of-pearl silk blouse that she packed for possible job interviews being dragged along on the floor.

In the wagon there is no space to sit. There are air holes running along the top of the train's sides. Everyone has turned their face upwards in the hope of catching a fresh breeze. The train jolts and shakes but there is no space to fall. The only thing that is shoved around at their feet is the metal bucket. Initially no one uses it – after all, the journey should only take a couple of hours – but then the train halts for ages in open fields. The doors remain closed in case it begins to move again. First the children use the bucket, afterwards the men and eventually the women too, peeing into it while standing.

To begin with Trude is still trying to think of what they will do once they reach Berlin. And she hopes they will return soon: she doesn't want Albert coming home to an empty place. But even these thoughts eventually stop and all she wants is for them just to endure the journey. Every now and again she quietly asks, 'Mum?' Agatha replies with a 'Hm.' Peter is standing between the two women, his cheek against his mother's stomach. Trude feels him breathing. A couple of times she nearly dozes off, but then with a start she regains consciousness. 'Mum?' 'Hm.' And she feels the breathing of her son.

And so it was that Agatha, Trude and Peter became part of the 11 million Germans who were fleeing westward in the winter of 1945. None of them knew where they were heading. But they all hoped to return home soon. Little did they know that the world was changing behind them and borders were being redrawn. Their homes now belonged to others and they were crossing into a foreign land.

The Red Shoes

TRUDE PUSHES ASIDE the thick curtain and looks out on to an empty stage. The music is playing. She knows she is on next. She strokes her tutu, shakes her arms gently to loosen them up. She goes up on pointe, places her arms into position by her side, tilts her head so that her face points to the left, in the direction of the audience, and then she is onstage. She moves in a line of female dancers. At the other end her fellow dancers disappear offstage. Trude will now perform her solo act. Only – suddenly she is aware that she has forgotten the movements. For a split second panic grips her, until she reminds herself that her body will know. And she lets go of all the tension and starts to move again. The music blows her across the boards. She is a dancer. And yet she isn't. Because all she does is let herself be carried by the waves of music. When they rise she is lifted, when they fall she is lowered. Sometimes the waves are long and she floats on their backs for quite a while, crossing the stage, owning the space. And sometimes they are short, arriving in quick succession, and she is surprised how calmly her body adapts to their rapid movements, their rapid cycles.

When she awakes the dream is as vivid in her mind as if she had just physically experienced it. For a moment she lies very still, before letting her hands glide across her body, checking if she is wearing a tutu. Fugitively, furtively; she doesn't want Peter to wake up. He is sharing her bed, lying head to toe. She returns her hands to the side of her body and would love to go back to the dream. What a beautiful light feeling. And she's never been on stage in her life. She smiles. But she would have loved to as a small girl.

She used to hide an old faded photograph of a beautiful ballerina in a metal box behind the chicken coop at the bottom of the garden, where she knew her mother would never look. Such a beautiful lady. 'From Paris,' her friend Ilse had told her. Ilse's uncle had been to Paris. Trude, too, wanted to go to Paris and become a ballerina.

She mentioned it once at the table to her mother, who told her off straight away: 'Where do you get such unclean ideas from?' And Agatha made the girl wash out her mouth with soap.

'Why am I unclean?' Trude asked her mother the next day.

'You are not unclean. Ballerinas are unclean.'

'But why?'

The lady in the photograph looked very beautiful and nice and clean. And elegant.

'A ballerina shows her knees and paints her lips red and dances on stage in front of men. A Pomeranian girl doesn't behave in such a way.'

Trude did make it to Paris. With Albert. But she has never danced on stage. In fact, until this dream she had forgotten about the photograph of the ballerina in the metal box. She hadn't thought about it since she was a girl. One day she just stopped going to the secret hiding spot behind the chicken coop. It was indeed dirty. She always ended up with lots of black earth underneath her fingernails. And that certainly was not appropriate for a fine lady.

Trude rolls quietly out of bed. In the other bed her mother is still fast asleep. She fetches her clothes and the night bucket and walks outside. Behind the shack she dresses in the glorious morning sun. Leaning against the wall, she lights a cigarette and closes her eyes. The rays of sun stroke her face. Only for a moment. She opens her eyes, extinguishes the half-smoked cigarette and puts it into her skirt pocket for later. She picks up the bucket and walks with it to the communal earth closet at the end of the lane. She leaves the empty bucket for her mother and Peter outside their shack. Trude is now in a hurry. She walks out of the camp and along the road to town. An army truck passes her and slows down, waiting for her. There are women in the back. They are probably heading to the market. Trude scans their faces. She doesn't recognize any of them. She shakes her head.

'No thanks. It's a beautiful morning. I will walk.'

She is walking fast, taking off her cardigan. In the field on her right cranes are stretching their necks. They have returned with the first warm spell of the year.

She falls into a trot. She doesn't want to be late. They meet at seven every Saturday morning in the church hall, Gerda said. They have two uninterrupted hours and it's a time that suits most of them. For the ones working in the fields, it's their day off, and the night-shifters from the cleaning team, like Trude, finish at three each morning anyway.

She arrives out of breath, sweat trickling down her temples. Before she opens the door, she wipes her face with the cardigan. The door squeaks loudly. Gerda is addressing a group of women sitting on the stage. She stops mid-sentence, turns around and flashes Trude a smile.

'Delighted you can join us.'

Trude makes her way to the front and up the small staircase at the side of the stage. Her heart beats like a little child's, as if she is about to perform.

'Ladies, take off your socks and shoes. The French can-can is best practised barefoot. Once we know what we are doing, we will go up on high heels,' Gerda announces.

After their practice the women visit the café for a cup of coffee and a schnapps. Gerda pays for Trude because she didn't bring her purse.

'To celebrate your first time.'

Later, at the town hall, like every Saturday, Trude scans the Red Cross list, her finger running down the columns. It's updated every week with the names of the released POWs who are searching for their displaced families. Trude too has put her name and their new home – a refugee camp in a small town near Hamburg – on numerous lists.

She always starts with 'A', even though the surnames appear first, so she could just check 'L'. But she doesn't. She goes through the letters twice, first searching for 'Lange', then for 'Albert'. After all, there could be a mistake. As she runs her finger and eyes up and down the columns, she feels neither hope nor despair. She's simply waiting. Waiting for Albert to return.

The shoes prove the most difficult part of the costume. Not least because they all agree that a French can-can without red high-heeled shoes is just not possible. They might as well not dance at all. But where to find eight pairs of red high-heeled shoes, considering that none of the women has any money to spare and there isn't much in the shops anyway. There is a thriving black market, though.

'The Tommies could surely help,' Irene sighs.

'How?' Lotte rolls her eyes at the silly suggestion.

'If they have silk stockings for us German ladies, they will be able to provide red dancing shoes,' Marlies throws in.

'For a price, that's for sure,' Elsbeth says, winking at Marlies.

'Their reward: watching us lift our skirts and throw up our stunning German legs with high-heeled red shoes sparkling on our feet. Highway to heaven,' Irmgard states coolly, and everyone bursts out laughing, until Gerda raises a hand.

'Excuse me, ladies, for interrupting your party, but dreaming about Tommies will not get us our red shoes. Can anyone come up with a more sensible suggestion?'

There is silence. All of them stare into their empty coffee cups.

'Actually, I can,' Trude says quietly.

All heads instantly turn towards her, a couple of eyebrows raised. But no one dares to interrupt with an inappropriate remark.

'I will meet my contact later today,' she continues. 'I can talk to him about the red shoes and see what he says.'

For half a minute or so the group is speechless.

'Well done, girl.' Gerda is the first to react. She leans across the table and squeezes Trude's hand.

The butcher doesn't know she's married. Christian Schmidt is his name.

The bell above the door rings as she steps into the shop. Their eyes meet for a fleeting second as he lifts his glance from

80

the cold meat he is cutting, letting his eyes wander above the customer's head towards the door, towards Trude.

'*Guten Tag.*'

'*Guten Tag.*'

A brief nod of recognition from both sides.

She sits down on the chair by the window. She usually comes earlier.

'Just a moment.' The butcher once again nods, with a brief smile to the other customer. He puts down the carving knife, wipes his hands on his apron and takes the big keyring from the shelf behind him.

'I will let you out, *meine Damen*, but it's one o'clock and on Saturdays we close at one.'

He locks the door and leaves the key inside. Then he turns the sign at the door to 'Closed'. Trude has picked up a magazine from the windowsill and is fanning herself.

'Would you like a glass of water?'

'Yes, please.'

He hurries around the corner and through a door into the back room. The woman left standing by the counter turns around, scrutinizing Trude impatiently. She's an elegant lady in a beautiful light green coat over a beige dress. Trude, on the other hand, wears an old dark green cotton dress that she picked up from a Red Cross collection a few weeks ago and which Agatha had to tighten in the back. Over it she wears her only brown cardigan, which frills at the wrists. Trude returns the woman's gaze with a smile. She has taught herself not to avert her eyes in situations like this. Friendly but firm. And certainly not apologetic. That seems to work best. The woman turns back to the counter and studies the meat display. Christian reappears and hands Trude a glass of water. Her fingers briefly touch his.

She's seen him receiving more money than a couple of sausages merit before and then handing back no change but instead a package he's fetched from the back room. As for Trude herself, he's given her minced meat and blood sausages and liver sausages. She always pays him something – one or two marks. And the kilo of minced meat he gave her only last week because there was no one else in the shop at that moment. If there are other people queuing up behind her he just adds more of what she's asked for. And she always asks for very little.

The woman pays. He passes her the paper-wrapped meat over the counter and she puts it into her shopping bag. Trude has emptied the glass and stands up. Christian hurries to open the door. When the customer has left, he locks it again. Trude listens. He doesn't pull the key out. She's relieved. If she has to get out, she can. He's a nice young man and so far his behaviour has been impeccable, but she's stringing him along. And that's always a dangerous game to play.

Christian has moved back to his place behind the counter. Trude didn't expect that. She anticipated that he would find a reason to stand next to her, albeit briefly. Maybe showing her some new cuts in his display.

She stretches out her hand with the water glass. 'I'd like some more water, please.' His hand clutches the glass. His fingertips over hers. She does not let go. He does not pull. Their eyes meet. He has beautiful blue eyes, a strong healthy jawline.

She fell right in front of his shop. It was past six o'clock. She was in a hurry because her shift starts at 6:30 every evening.

She lay on the ground, not moving for a moment, paralysed by the stinging pain in her nose. Had she broken it? Tears shot into her eyes. While she was falling, she had put her hands out in an attempt to stop her face slamming down. She tasted dirt in her mouth.

'Are you OK?'

Someone was kneeling next to her. She lifted her head, saw a man's shoes. She tried to raise herself up, but the palms of her hands were burning badly.

'May I help you?'

The man's voice was deep and calm. She nodded. He supported her lower arms while she stood up. It was the butcher. He bent down and gathered up the bag with her sandwich for her tea break at eleven. She saw her grazed knees, her grazed hands. She didn't dare to touch her nose. She ran her tongue along her gums. Her teeth seemed fine and she didn't taste any blood in amongst the dirt in her mouth. He held out her bag and she took it without looking him in the eyes.

'Thank you,' she mumbled. She stepped aside in order to walk around him. Instantly she felt dizzy, swaying slightly; she stopped to regain her balance.

'Let me accompany you home,' she heard the man say. She shook her head.

'No, no. I'll be fine.'

'Then rest a minute or two while I check to see how badly you're hurt.'

As he was speaking, he approached the door of his shop and was now pointing inside. He leaned forward and pulled the chair into the doorway, turning it to face the street. Trude hadn't yet attempted to move again. Her head was spinning, but she just wanted to get to work on time. It was a miracle that she had secured a job with the cleaning team in the first place. She couldn't afford to lose it. But perhaps a glass of water would do her good. Once again she nodded. He touched her elbow lightly and guided her to the chair, then disappeared inside the shop. A couple of people passed her, staring. She got up and moved the chair back inside, but left the door open. The butcher returned with a wet cotton cloth and some bandages.

'We should clean your wounds,' he said.

'No, no, please don't worry.' She felt sick.

'It won't take a moment. I have everything here.'

He was kneeling down beside her, cleaning the wounds on her knees, on her hands. His hands were big and strong.

'May I?'

She nodded.

He took her jaw in his hand and turned her face towards him. They were so close she could feel his breath on her skin. It was a warm smell.

She removed his hand and stood up.

'I need to get going.'

She went back. The first time because she hadn't said thank you. She didn't want him to think her impolite. At least that's what she told herself. After all, it was obvious she was a refugee. The next time she returned she had two marks to buy a couple of sausages for their soup. He gave her five. She didn't know until she opened the package back in the shack. She noticed he didn't wear a wedding ring. But he was young, maybe too young to be married. Then again, she didn't wear one either. In her case she had bought penicillin for Peter with it on the black market last winter. And her diamond ring she had hidden in the hole underneath the floorboards. It was now the only health insurance they had left, the brooch and necklace long gone: one traded to cross into the British sector in the summer of '45, and the pearls of the necklace exchanged one by one for food in that first harsh winter of '45/'46.

Almost imperceptibly, Trude pushes the glass firmly into Christian's hand and pulls her fingers from underneath his. Her eyes on his. On her way here she opened the top button of her blouse.

He returns with the water glass filled once again, this time walking around the counter and coming to stand right in front of her. She takes the glass, without touching his fingers.

'I have to lower the blinds.'

The street outside is empty. It's lunchtime. Everyone has gone home. No one knows that she is here. He lowers the blinds in front of the big window. He lowers the blind in front of the door.

Trude has observed him for weeks: he's not a flirt. She has fantasized about making love to him against the counter, going upstairs with him to his place, where he would slowly undress her and cover her entire body with kisses. She has imagined his firm, healthy body in her arms, above her, beneath her.

He's walking towards her now. She hasn't moved.

Just kissing. Maybe just kissing. And running her hands through the short hair at the back of his head.

He's standing in front of her now.

No. Her body wants more. Her body wants all of him. Her body won't let her stop at kissing.

He takes the glass out of her hand.

She's always imagined herself the princess waiting for the prince to kiss her. As she stands in front of Christian, she now knows that she is no longer a princess and he's no prince. And he won't kiss her. She will have to kiss him.

He's holding the glass with both hands. Looking into it. Like a clumsy boy. Trude feels a laugh rising up from her belly into her throat. She wants a man, not a boy.

'Can you get me eight pairs of red high-heeled shoes? We can pay.'

He lifts his glance, looking straight into her eyes. She holds his stare unblinkingly.

'Is that why you came?' He clears his throat.

'Yes.' A harsh sound. She didn't mean to sound so harsh.

The right corner of his mouth twitches and he turns towards the counter, putting the glass down.

'Yes, I can.'

'Soon?'

'How soon do you need them?'

'Three weeks?'

His right hand is still on the glass. For a moment he is silent.

'Yes. But it will cost you.'

'How much?'

She hasn't taken her eyes off him. He's now moving his hand away from the glass and turning his back towards her, walking to the other side of the room, to the end of the counter, then behind the counter. She feels him straighten up, his shoulders suddenly broader again.

'How many pairs did you say?' He begins to undo the buttons on his white coat.

'Eight.'

He takes his coat off and hangs it on a hook. He rolls up the sleeves of his shirt, still half turned away from her. She watches his big hands, observes the protruding veins on his lower arms twitching.

'A piece of jewellery for each one, gold at least, no wedding rings. And I need them by Tuesday if you want the shoes within the next three weeks.'

He has finished rolling up his sleeves and is now heading towards the door.

'I'll let you out.'

No, he is no prince, and she is no princess. Trude still doesn't move. He has arrived at the door, reaches out to turn the key. She didn't just come because of the red shoes. He pushes the door handle and opens the door.

'I'll see you Tuesday then.'

He stands by the door as if waiting to usher her out. As her legs finally begin to move, the heat rises to her cheeks. She's misinterpreted his body language. Of course! Shame envelops her like a sudden fog. He's probably barely over twenty. Just a few years older than Peter. How could she? She nods silently as she passes him. In his eyes she must be an old woman – an old, gaunt refugee woman with thin hair and bad skin. The bright sun illuminates the empty pavement. She turns left, not speeding up, not slowing down. She reaches the end of the road. She stops mid-stride. Her body might be marked by years of hunger and deprivation, but it can still pick up on signs when a man wants her. All it required was for her to take the initiative. To kiss him. She looks back over her shoulder. She can't see Christian, but she can see the door standing ajar.

She tells the girls the following day that they can have their red shoes. They called an emergency meeting just before the night shift.

'With high heels?'

'Yes.'

'In the right sizes?'

'Yes, he wants me to give him our sizes.'

'When will we get our shoes?'

'A week before our performance, so we have time to practise in them.'

Cheering breaks out.

'Shh, be quiet. We don't want to draw attention to ourselves.'

They return to a whisper.

'What will it cost?'

Trude looks down at the hole in her right shoe where her dirty big toe shows.

'A piece of jewellery from each of us,' she says hoarsely.

Unanimous sharp intake of breath. Silence.

'How does he know?' Marlies asks with barely concealed suspicion in her voice.

'They know,' Gerda hisses. She feels protective towards Trude. 'Everyone knows that we sewed our valuables inside our winter coats as we fled. But what they don't know is where we've hidden them since.'

'I tried to dissuade him from the idea,' Trude murmurs, barely audible, digging her naked toe into the dust in front of her. 'But he was adamant. It's the only payment that would encourage his contact in London to act swiftly enough on the order. He personally would not ask for such payment from us, he said. He knows how little we have and that we have lost everything else that reminds us of home. But he also said that the English aristocracy love old German jewellery. Best craftsmanship available.'

Trude falls silent suddenly, as if she has already said too much.

Irene pulls out a packet of cigarettes from her skirt pocket, lights one and hands it to Trude.

'You've done well, girl.'

She lights another cigarette for herself and blows out the smoke. 'Better than any of us,' she adds. 'And now, ladies, it's up to us. What do we want to do? We now know the price. We have two options: either we say it's too high, we won't pay it, and dance barefoot like poor homeless harlots, or—' she pauses and takes another drag on her cigarette '—we pay the price and we feel like proud women in high heels and give a performance that no one will ever forget. And as an added bonus we will all go back to our miserable huts and wake up the next morning with a pair of red shoes underneath our bed.'

The cawing of a crow interrupts the stillness that follows. When it has stopped, Trude says, 'He needs to have the jewellery by Tuesday. Otherwise there won't be enough time. I've arranged to meet him after my shift.'

They avoid each other's eyes. The three who still have their wedding rings think the same: they will give the ring.

Trude drops her cigarette butt. 'No wedding rings, he said.'

'Is that a joke?' Elsbeth calls out.

Gerda steps forward and grabs her hard by the arm. 'Pull yourself together, Elsbeth.'

'Of course, no wedding rings.' Elsbeth frees her arm from Gerda's grip with one swift, strong movement. 'That's fine for the slut, isn't it just?'

Gerda interrupts quickly: 'Be quiet. Otherwise you are out.'

They stand motionless for a few seconds while the rest hold their breath.

'I have a watch on a golden chain. It used to belong to my grandfather,' Elsbeth then declares, looking defiantly at each of the other women in turn and finally coming to rest again on Gerda.

'I have a short pearl necklace with a diamond lock from my mother,' Gerda offers calmly and without hesitation.

And so each of them takes her turn. Trude puts forward her diamond ring.

Elsbeth nods briefly in Trude's direction. 'What guarantee do we have that she won't bag our jewellery and skip off over the mountains with her handsome *contact*' – she sneers at that word – 'to live happily ever after?'

'None,' Gerda replies. And she now turns to look Trude straight in the face. 'But if anything goes wrong with this deal, her family will pay dearly. Do we understand each other?'

Gerda is the only one of the women who killed her rapists.

They were a group of women and children and old people. Agatha, Trude and Peter had joined the group sometime in May '45, somewhere near Grimmen. They had found a deserted farmhouse for the night. Gerda was supposed to keep guard upstairs while the others slept in the cellar. But she too must have fallen asleep. She awoke when they lifted her up on to the kitchen table. Four Russian soldiers. They were so drunk they fell asleep as soon as they had had their way with her. The last one didn't even close his flies. Gerda got up from the table and pulled down her skirt. She removed her boots quietly. Carefully she stepped over the sleeping bodies and went across to the guns that were leaning against the wall. It struck her what a pathetic straight line the guns had been arranged in. She picked up two, one in each hand, carried them down the corridor and put them in front of the closed cellar door. Then she headed back into the kitchen. The soldiers hadn't stirred. She picked up the remaining two guns and walked out of the kitchen again. She left one next to the other two. With the fourth gun in her hand, she returned to the soldiers. Her brother had taught her to shoot. She stood over the first one and aimed straight at his heart. She knew that once she had fired the first shot she would have only a split seconds for the other three, as they would be roused by the noise. Luckily, they were drunk. She smiled as she fired. Blood sprayed up. But she had already turned to his sleeping comrade. And then the next one. The fourth had started to stir, the one with open trousers. She pointed the gun between his legs and watched his face change from childlike incomprehension to an expression of utter horror. She was about to pull the trigger.

'That's enough, Gerda,' she heard Trude say.

She hesitated, her finger on the trigger. The soldier stood frozen in front of her, both arms up in the air. Trude placed her hand gently on Gerda's.

'Let go, Gerda.'

Trude fastened her grip around Gerda's hand. They remained in this position, motionless, perhaps for a second, perhaps for an eternity. Eventually Gerda could feel Trude's touch and let her guide her hand away from the trigger, let her take the gun. The soldier turned and ran.

Neither Trude nor Gerda ever told anyone about that incident.

❦

Trude now whispers, 'I understand.'

'Good.' Gerda nods. 'Let's all meet here again tomorrow at the same time.'

Trude shuts the door quietly behind her and waits till her eyes have adapted to the dark. She listens to Peter and her mother breathing. They are fast asleep. Nevertheless, she decides not to fetch the ring straight away. Usually her mother wakes up around this hour, knowing that Trude is returning, but this time Trude wants to make sure that her mother is sound asleep.

Agatha risked her life for this ring. In the summer of 1945 they passed through many checkpoints, and since they had no possessions left they usually walked straight through. But eventually they came to one where every refugee was shaken down. Until that day Agatha had never let her winter coat out of her sight. But as word was spreading among the refugees that at this checkpoint they were more thorough than elsewhere, Agatha decided to hide the jewellery in a different place.

Trude begged her mother not to do it. 'They are searching everywhere.'

'They only do spot searches down there on young women,' Agatha replied, stony-faced.

The soldier took Agatha's coat. Trude's heart stopped. Surely he would notice the holes in the lining where the jewellery used to be hidden. They knew the tricks as well as everyone else. But Agatha had detached the entire lining so skilfully that the soldier couldn't tell the coat had ever had a lining in the first place.

Trude takes off her shoes but keeps her skirt and blouse

on. She slips into bed next to Peter, who mumbles something and turns to the wall, his feet nearly kicking his mother's face. He is growing fast. Soon it will no longer be appropriate for him to share the bed with her. Trude folds her hands over her stomach and feels them lifting up and down to the rhythm of her breathing. A mosquito is buzzing over Agatha's bed. Then silence. Then a smack on naked skin. Trude closes her eyes. She feels Peter climbing over her and out of bed. Pee is running into the bucket.

'Mum?'

'Hm?'

'You shouldn't sleep in your clothes,' Peter whispers.

'I won't,' Trude mumbles. 'Go back to sleep.'

Silence returns to the room. The mosquito keeps quiet too. Agatha must have killed it.

Trude suddenly opens her eyes with a start. Outside a grey dawn is breaking. She gets up quickly and silently. She has no time to lose. She rushes to the corner next to the door where the wooden crate with their few belongings stands. She doesn't risk pushing it for fear of scraping noises that might wake the others. She lifts it and carries it to the middle of the room. She goes down on her knees and removes a nail that is stuck loosely in one of the floorboards. Then she removes the floorboard. Underneath it plain earth becomes apparent. She fetches a spoon from the crockery shelf and starts digging. She has to reach deeper than she remembers. She hid it well. But eventually she hits the little parcel wrapped in linen cloth. She opens it. A photo of her and Albert lies on top. The only thing Agatha managed to hold on to when the entire contents of the suitcase spilled on to the platform in Stettin. Trude stares at the picture. The two figures appear like ghosts from another world. She slides the ring into her pocket without looking at it. Then she wraps up the photograph again, returns it to its hiding place, uses her bare hands to cover it with earth and restores the floorboard to its proper place. As she straightens up her gaze meets Agatha's wide-open eyes. Her mother is lying on her side, her hands resting beneath her left cheek. The whites of Agatha's eyes shine as bright as a light. Trude turns away, picks up her shoes and leaves the room, pulling the door quietly shut behind her.

Of course Agatha was not happy about Trude's frivolous stage dream, and she was even more unhappy about her daughter trading their last piece of jewellery, their last piece of health insurance. But then it occurred to Agatha that giving away Albert's ring was a sign that Trude was letting go, was ready to move on. Ever since they had arrived in the West, Agatha had tried to persuade Trude to declare Albert dead so that she'd be able to claim a widow's pension that would allow them to move out of the camp more quickly. A lot of women did that. But Trude had so far resisted. She didn't want to tempt fate.

So maybe Trude was now ready to let go of the hope of ever seeing Albert again. And maybe she wasn't. We will never know. However, what we do know is that Albert was released from Russian captivity in early spring 1947 and informed the Red Cross of his whereabouts. He did not know where his family was. But he, like Trude, had never given up hope.

PART III: REFUGE

The Return of the Soldier

THE TRAIN PULLS up at the station. Thick smoke envelops the platform. Doors are opening, people are rushing out. Some are greeted while others walk away with heads held low. The conductor blows his whistle, the wheels begin to move again, the train leaves the station.

When crowd and smoke have cleared, the outline of a man appears, standing motionless, a little suitcase in one hand and his hat in the other. He bends his knees, puts his suitcase down. He places his hat on his head and adjusts it with both hands. Once he has secured it at the right angle, he picks up his case and, with a swinging step, strolls along, humming quietly to himself. No melody in particular, just a lovely light tune.

Opposite the train station he spots a café with a free table outside in the sun. He orders a coffee, lights a cigarette, leans back and blows perfect smoke rings into the air.

When his cigarette is finished, Albert pushes the coffee cup to one side and lifts the suitcase on to the table. It contains only two objects of importance, plus three packets of chewing gum. Carefully he takes out the parcel wrapped in a piece of old curtain and folds back the fabric. It's a Leica from before the war. He got it for next to nothing; no one is interested in that sort of stuff at the moment. He holds it in his hands like a delicate glass bowl that might break at a firmer touch. He has repaired it, even managed to replace a couple of screws, cleaned it. He polished the little silver parts. And he bought a film. He slides his hand inside his trouser pocket where he keeps it so it won't accidentally fall out of the suitcase. He hasn't yet taken pictures with the camera but he knows the mechanics of it inside out; he's confident it's working. He places it back into the fabric. He unwraps the second parcel and gently strokes the picture frame that holds three perfectly dried buttercups. He dried them himself. Will Trude still remember? And for Peter he bought three packets of chewing gum. Any boy likes chewing gum.

After putting everything back into the suitcase and closing it, he waves to the waiter and pays. His last money. He stands up, shakes his legs and pulls his trousers and matching suit jacket straight. Oh yes, he's wearing a suit. He's still the man he used to be. He's left nothing to chance.

Albert strolls along. He's in no hurry. Trude knows he will arrive this week. But she doesn't know which day. The Red Cross found her four weeks ago when he was still in hospital, where they managed to restore him so he now has enough weight on him to walk upright.

He's humming once again. He's trying to think about good things. The blue sky. The beautiful feeling of just walking along a road, with a hat on your head and a suitcase full of presents in your hand. He's never returned from his travels empty-handed. He always brought gifts home. A man of the world.

He can now see the camp from afar. He's sweating. He's pushing his hat back, pulling out his handkerchief, dabbing his forehead. He doesn't know what time it is. It must be past five o'clock. Maybe close to six. He stops, waiting for his heartbeat to calm. It might be beating so hard because of the heat and the walking, or because he's about to see Trude and Peter again.

In the camp he's pointed the right way. Eyes are following him. Everyone knows that he's expected. He can see the door of their shack standing ajar. He waits outside, listens. No sound. He knocks. A chair is pushed back. The door opens.

A blond twelve-year-old boy is standing in front of him. Man and boy look at each other. The boy can't remember ever having seen a photograph of his father. The man can't remember that that's what his son looked like. He once had a photograph of himself with his wife and child, but he lost it or someone took it away.

Albert stretches out his hand.

'Peter?' The boy nods. 'I'm your father.'

The boy shakes Albert's hand. A firm handshake.

'*Guten Abend.*'

Peter can't really bring himself to call this man 'Papa'. He imagined his father to be broader. He's got a vague memory of his parents dancing to the radio in the sitting room. And in this memory his father looks strong. This man is tall and very thin, his cheeks sunken. If only his mother, or at least his grandmother, was here. For all he knows this could be anyone. Although, of course, he was aware that his father was coming.

The boy has pulled his hand out of Albert's. But he doesn't appear to be wanting to move.

'Can I come in?' Albert asks.

Peter jumps as if startled and steps aside. He points to the table and his chair.

Albert takes off his hat. Part of him would just love to hug the boy. To press the boy, his boy, against him. To feel him. Breathing. His heartbeat. But there is no way he can do that. Everything about the boy tells him to keep his distance.

Albert sits down at the table while Peter is moving around to the other side. He has left the door open. Albert looks round and Peter follows his glance.

'We only have one chair,' he says. Then adds quickly, 'Do you want some water?'

Albert nods. 'Yes, please.'

Peter takes the cup and the saucepan that are standing on the table and fills the cup.

'Is this your homework?' Albert points with a nod of his head to the open book on the table. It's a book about boxing, from what he can make out.

Peter shakes his head. 'No. My trainer lent me the book. I'm boxing in a club.'

The boy's glance wanders to the left, to the only shelf in the room. Next to the sparse crockery stands the trophy he won two weeks ago in the area's championship for the under-twelves. His first ever trophy. He's allowed to keep it for an entire year, then he must hand it to the next winner.

Albert turns a few pages, looking at the photographs and drawings that explain different fighting and punching techniques. An image of a man's face being punched underneath the chin, the head tilted backwards, catches his eye. He closes the book, pushes it away.

'When did you start boxing?'

'When I was small,' Peter says, leaning across the table, picking up the book. 'I need to go now. Training starts at six.' He's already half out of the door when he turns around, clutching the book to his chest with both arms.

'Grandma will be back soon. And Mum's shift is just about to start.'

Albert is heading out of the camp again, with his suitcase in his hand. It didn't feel right to leave it. His strides are long. He's keeping his gaze directed a couple of metres in front of his feet. He has a purpose. He doesn't want to meet Agatha. He wants to meet Trude. Peter explained to him where she works. He will wait for her. He's still got a packet of cigarettes. That'll do. He's become good at waiting. And eight and a half hours is nothing.

Albert has now left the camp behind. He slows his pace. He begins to hum that tune again, ambling along. He's got plenty of time.

She punches her card out and turns to see a figure in a hat standing on the other side of the road. And even though she can't see his face, only the dark outline, she knows it is him. Because of the hat. The way that hat sits on the head. At a slight angle to the left. He's leaning against a wall, a little suitcase standing next to him, one leg raised, foot flat against the wall. The glimmer of a cigarette in his hand. For a moment she stops. She isn't wearing her high-heeled red shoes! Ever since she's known that Albert is coming back, she's imagined meeting him in her red shoes.

'Is that Albert?' Gerda has appeared next to Trude. Other women are rushing past, wanting to get to their beds as quickly as possible.

Trude nods. Gerda squeezes her friend's shoulder briefly before she walks off.

The figure opposite has now dropped his

cigarette. He takes his foot from the wall and straightens up.

Trude walks over slowly. She stretches out her arms and lifts them and pulls his hat down over his forehead as she used to do.

'You're back,' she says. And she puts her arms around his waist and her head against his shoulder. He's become so thin, her Albert.

Lips on lips.

She pushes herself away from him. She places her palms gently on his chest, slowly moving them down towards his waistband. Her eyes follow her hands. For a brief moment she feels his abdominals tensing beneath her fingers. Her hands glide towards his hips, sensing the slight curve before they move on to his back. Her fingertips feel the indentation of his spine.

She hears his heart beating, his shallow breathing. But he doesn't move, doesn't say a word. Trude pulls his shirt out of the back of his trousers and pushes her hands underneath it. Skin. The warmth of naked, living skin. She rests her cheek on his shoulder, inhaling deeply. The pressure of her hands on his back increases. She feels his hands on her hips. She pulls her hands from underneath his shirt and moves a couple of steps back. She takes off her cardigan and takes off her dress, she unhooks her bra and steps out of her pants, all the while not letting go of Albert's eyes with her own. Her Albert's eyes. They are still the same. Then she steps forward, releasing his face, concentrating on the buttons of his shirt, opening them, sliding the shirt from his shoulders, down his back, his arms, his hands. She unbuckles his belt, opens his trousers. She squats and helps him step out of his trousers, his pants, his socks.

She places the tips of her right index and middle finger on his chest, his heartbeat vibrating against the skin, and lets them travel downwards towards his belly button. His hands on her hips again, light, without any pressure. She feels them shaking, steps closer and feels his firmness. His softness. And closes her eyes.

He takes her hand. She keeps her eyes closed. She can smell him in the darkness. She's smiling to herself. She mustn't open her eyes or else the spell might break and everything that is suddenly so near will be over. His lips on hers, on her neck, her breasts, her belly, her thighs. His hands on her body, stroking, dancing over her arms, her hips, her back, her behind. She feels Albert breathing inside her. And she feels the fluttering in her stomach, in her head. Her feet lift off the ground, her body lifts off the ground and her mind becomes as light as a beautiful summer cloud. And she's finally once again hovering in the air, swirling around. Feeling her body alive.

They are lying naked on the bed that Albert shares with Peter. The other bed, which Trude and her mother share, is pushed up against the door of their shack. It's Saturday morning, a few days after Albert's return. It's the first time Trude and Albert have been alone. Peter is at school, Agatha has gone to the market.

'Do you remember how we always talked about going to America when the war was over?' Trude smiles. 'We've made it to the North Sea now. We're on our way.'

Albert has turned his head to the other side to stub out his cigarette. A rat that is running across the floor disappears into a hole in the wall on the other side.

'And we have company too,' he laughs.

'Eeh, Albert, don't point them out to me.' Trude playfully rolls half on to her husband.

Trude and Albert are quiet.

'Put your arms around me,' Trude murmurs after a while.

Albert lifts his arms and wraps them around Trude's back. Her cheek is resting on his shoulder. Instinctively, he places his cheek on the top of her head. Too late he realizes that he shouldn't have done that.

A sharp pain rips through his chest.

This is how he used to lie with her many, many years ago. In another life, in another world. He'd buried the memory of Trude's head on his shoulder, buried it deep, very deep, to protect it; didn't even realize it was still there. But now it had resurfaced, and all the missing moments that they would have spent together – Trude's head on his shoulder and his cheek on her head – if the war hadn't intervened are coming back to stab him in the heart with their irreversible absence. Again and again and again. And there is nothing he can do except lie here and let it happen.

He tries not to move, to endure the pain without letting Trude know that is ripping him apart. He doesn't want her to know because the place where the pain comes from – all those years spent far, far away – has nothing to do with her. And has nothing to do with him, the real Albert, either.

He's back now.

'What happened to you?' he hears Trude whisper.

And he tells her about his luck. The commander of his battalion was obsessed with documenting the war: 'To show our children in years to come how it all began, how we fought and suffered to become rulers of the world.' When the photographer was killed, Albert stepped forward and gave his credentials. The commander was impressed, and from then on Albert was the official war photographer of the battalion.

He was asked to take only heroic pictures. And so he did. He does not tell Trude that 'heroic' pictures also meant depicting hanged civilians and burnt villages and mutilated enemy soldiers.

He was indeed lucky. While before the war the camera was his extended eye, which he used to capture his view of the world, it was now what protected him, behind which he hid, which kept him, the real Albert, at a distance. Far, far away from everything that was happening around him.

It worked. Until he became a prisoner and they took away the camera and took away the picture of Trude in the buttercup dress standing in the buttercup meadow by the Madüsee back home.

Albert fetches his little suitcase and slides back on to the bed. Trude nestles up close to him as he lifts the lid.

'I brought gifts for you and Peter.'

He watches her face as she opens the present. It only takes her a moment to understand the meaning of the three buttercups. Tears come to her eyes.

'Oh, Albert!'

He shows her the camera. Now it is her turn to watch his face. Albert's eyes shine like those of a little boy as he explains how well he's fixed the camera.

'I can't wait to show Peter how to take photos.'

He bends closer to open the film compartment, looks inside, blows into it – just in case there might be some dust.

'Take a picture of the two of us like you used to do with your arm outstretched,' Trude tries to encourage him.

'No, not in here.' He closes the film compartment with a firm push. 'The light isn't good,' he adds in a slightly milder tone.

Trude is sitting on the crossbar, Alfred is pedalling. He's getting stronger by the day.

And look at him! His first week's pay is in his pocket. He's riding his own bicycle. And a beautiful woman is sitting in front of him on the crossbar for everyone to see, her blonde hair blowing in his face, her red lips smiling. Yes, he is a lucky man. He got a job at the mill. Hard, physical work, but he was already able to demonstrate his accounting skills to the miller. After all, he ran his own business for many years. And the miller has hinted that he might need more help in the office. And then the bicycle! Albert can't believe his luck. He's the proud owner of a bicycle.

Albert and Trude are now walking up the dyke, Albert pushing the bike. On the top they stop suddenly.

'Where is the sea?' Albert leans over the handlebars, catching his breath while squinting.

In front of them, at the bottom of the sea-facing side of the dyke, there is nothing but mudflats reaching all the way to the horizon. In the distance a couple of matchstick-sized people are walking.

'It's low tide,' Trude says, laughing. 'How amazing. I never knew that the sea could go out that far.'

Albert swings his leg over the saddle. 'Hop on.' He points with a nod of his head to the back carrier. 'And hold on tight.'

They cheer and shriek as they head down, faster and faster. Trude screws up her face against Albert's back in horror and delight.

'Albert, Albert, don't let us die,' she screeches, partly in earnest, partly not. Partly fearing it, partly not. Albert is back. Her Albert is back. And nothing much can go wrong now.

He brakes just in time and nearly flies over the handlebars, but then he feels his feet firmly planted on the ground. Trude has jumped off and appears in front of him, throwing her arms around his neck and pressing her lips against his.

'You're my hero,' she giggles.

They wonder what to do with the bike. They can't take it across the mud. And it's Albert's dearest possession. He travels to work on it every day. Then they look at each other like two naughty children, reading each other's minds. They lie down in the sun, waiting for the sea to come back. They have all the time in the world. It's their day off. No one is expecting them. Trude kicks off her red, high-heeled shoes. Lies back, folds her arms beneath her head. The sky above them is the bluest blue, as if it has never known any clouds. Ever.

'You should have brought your camera,' Trude says. 'The light is perfect.'

Albert pretends he didn't hear.

The first thing Albert did when he was discharged from hospital was to buy the Leica. Once he had repaired it, he put in the film, ready to take his first picture. He had promised himself one photograph only; the second one he wanted to take of Trude when they met again. In hospital he had walked, in his mind, streets and towns and fields and lanes looking for the perfect shot, his first shot in freedom. But then he realized that all his images and visions were of home, of a world that no longer existed. So he decided to think of a single object that he would photograph instead. It didn't take long, and he knew it had to be a buttercup. He found a field. He went down on his knees, leaned forward on his front arms and focused the camera. He put his eye to the lens. A bright yellow flower stared at him. It stung his eyes. He couldn't take the picture. He moved on to the next flower. And the next. He spent many hours looking for the perfect buttercup. A buttercup worthy of his shot, gentle on his eyes. But there were none. That's why he decided instead to pick three flowers and dry them to give them in a frame to Trude.

Then Albert began to imagine that if only he could teach his son the art of photography – how to look at the world in an aesthetically pleasing way – he himself might reconnect with this skill, the skill that the real Albert from before the war used to be such a master of.

But Peter was not interested in the camera. He was only interested in his boxing club. At first, when Albert returned, he knew he could not impose himself on the boy. He had to give Peter space and time to get to know him again. Oh, Albert did understand his son. Even understood his obsession with boxing, indeed the necessity of having boxed while his father was away. Handing out punches made the boy feel strong and tough, able to protect his mother and grandmother. Albert is proud of his son. But now he is back there is so much he wants to show him.

'I want Peter to stop boxing.'

Albert's glance is on the shelf with the framed buttercups and Peter's sparkling trophy. This trophy always seems to be sparkling, even when outside storm clouds are gathering. Every morning the boy polishes it with a special little handkerchief that he keeps folded under the mattress. The trophy is in the shape of a golden boxer holding one gloved hand up to his face and the other stretched out ready to punch.

Albert squints and the outlines disappear, dissolving into a nondescript object. He takes a final drag on his cigarette before stretching his right arm out to the floor in order to stub it out in the metal lid that serves as an ashtray. It's dark in the room. As if it were evening and not a Saturday morning – Albert and Trude's usual hour on their own. Big dark rain clouds are hanging over the camp. The wind has picked up too. Trude hears the poplars along the brook behind the camp whipping the air.

For a moment her head remains on Albert's shoulder. But she's suddenly aware that there hasn't yet been any thunder or lightning, and she sits up. Then she turns around, facing Albert, as she lowers herself on to her knees. She expected him to say something like this sooner or later.

'You know that Peter loves boxing. Even back home, when he was a small boy, that's what he wanted to become. Do you remember? You ignored it, saying it's just a phase any little boy goes through. Like wanting to be an engine driver.'

Thunder is now rumbling in the distance.

She leans forward and strokes Albert's hair away from his forehead. He looks exhausted.

'It's not a good sport for the boy. It's brutal and violent. It doesn't teach him the right values.' Albert moves his head so that Trude's hand falls away from his face. 'Leave it,' he says. Then: 'I don't recognize my boy.' Albert doesn't look at Trude. 'If I had been around I would have made sure that he didn't get caught up in something like this.'

He can hear her take a deep breath.

'It's the best thing that has happened to him, Albert.'

Trude's voice is stern, maybe too stern, and she softens it. 'It's his own thing. It connects him to home. And it integrates him here.' Then she suddenly laughs. 'You know what, you should come with me and watch him tomorrow afternoon. He's got a fight. And maybe you can bring your camera.' Once again she leans forward, wanting this time to take Albert's face between her two hands. 'It's only collecting dust at the moment, and that's a pity.'

With a quick movement of his arm, Albert prevents her from coming close. 'Don't! Don't keep touching my face.' Then he adds, 'If the boy wants to continue boxing, he also has to spend some time with me showing him how to take photos.'

He reaches for another cigarette. 'It's not about photography per se.' His voice is calmer now, as remorse climbs from his stomach to his throat. He is sorry for his outbreak of impatience with Trude – it isn't the first time, and that pains him. 'But it's the only thing I know and I'm really good at.' He smiles faintly. 'And it will show Peter something about the world around him other than violence and destruction.' He strikes the match.

Trude wraps her arms around her body. The approaching storm has cooled the air. An autumnal cold chill has entered the room. She wishes Albert would start taking photographs again. This idea that he only bought the camera to show Peter is downright silly. But she'll talk to the boy. He's sensible, and if it means father and son go out together looking for things to photograph, maybe that'll do them both good.

But what neither Albert nor Trude were aware of at that moment was that their son had begun to take his boxing skills out of the club and into the playground. He was fast becoming the talk of the town. It took Albert's boss, the miller, to reveal to Albert the fist-fighter his son had turned into.

'My son and yours know each other. They're in the same class at school.'

The miller, Heinrich Lemke, hands Albert a bottle of beer. The two men are sitting on wooden blocks outside the miller's office, facing each other. The other workers have already gone home for the day. A golden Indian summer's day is drawing to a close. Dusk is announcing the night's chill. Albert shivers. The sweat from a hard day's work is damp on his skin. He takes the cold bottle with a nod. He would have preferred a hot tea, but still he lifts the beer to his lips. He can't reject the miller's offer. It's the first time that Heinrich has invited him for a drink, clearly in the mood to chat. Albert doesn't want to disturb – or even upset – the atmosphere with unnecessary demands. He wants the miller to feel at ease in his company. The ice-cold liquid runs down Albert's throat and into his small, hollow belly. The alcohol won't do him any good. In the last few days his stomach has started to play up again, rejecting a lot of the stuff that it hasn't received over the previous years.

He waits. Takes another small sip. And another, wondering when he can put down the bottle and still look grateful. Eventually he spreads his legs and rests his arms on his thighs, dangling the beer between his fingers. He looks down and closes his eyes for a moment, hoping that the miller won't notice. His tummy makes a lot of noise, but the beer stays down.

The miller is chatting about the boys.

'My son's name is Karl. He's twelve, like yours. Karl's mentioned Peter a few times before, but it was only when he said that Peter's dad had recently rejoined his family that it clicked up here.' Heinrich taps his right index finger against his forehead. 'A good boxer apparently, your son.' He clinks his bottle against Albert's. 'Cheers.'

He likes the new guy. Hard-working, tries to fit in, not a complainer. After all, no one's lot – displaced or not – is easy. As Heinrich's lips close around the bottleneck, he notices his hand shaking. Quickly he changes hands and pretends to wipe a dirt mark off his trousers to cover up the trembling. It still sometimes happens out of the blue.

'New pair of trousers.' He laughs. 'My wife didn't want me to wear them to the mill. She'll get angry when she sees them dirty.'

Albert has straightened himself up, smiles back at the miller – without really understanding the relevance of his last comment – and takes another swig. He would love to get up now and go home, or even continue working. He feels safer working. Less can go wrong.

Heinrich suddenly places a hand on Albert's shoulder. 'You're OK?'

Instinctively, Albert's body tenses, but then he forces himself to relax so that the miller won't sense his unease.

'Yes, all OK.' He nods, clearing his throat, and starts to unwrap the sandwich that was left over from lunch. 'Peter has mentioned a boy named Karl a number of times,' he lies. The truth is Peter doesn't mention anyone from school. When he talks, he only talks about his boxing club. And his trainer. 'The two seem to be forging a friendship,' he continues. 'Karl has obviously made an impression on Peter.'

Albert bites carefully into the sandwich. Hopefully the bread will absorb the alcohol.

Heinrich rests his back against the wall of his office and folds his hands in front of his belly. With his beer between his palms, he closes his eyes. The shaking has subsided. It never lasts long, thanks to his self-control.

'Pleased to hear my son is finding his place among his schoolmates. At home he is often rather unimpressive.'

Not at all like his dead brother, Heinrich would like to add. He opens his eyes with a start. Why does he want to tell this newcomer, this stranger, his worker, about his eldest son? He needs to pull himself together.

'I've got a matter to discuss with you on behalf of the boys.' The miller's voice has turned stern.

Albert is suppressing a burp and swallows the sour slime that has come up.

'It appears that your son is causing trouble for himself in the schoolground, using his fists a bit too much and getting into fights with the local boys.'

Albert swallows the half-chewed lump of bread. 'I can talk to Peter,' he says, then starts to cough.

Heinrich bends forward, picks up Albert's bottle from the ground and holds it out to him. 'Drink.'

Albert tilts his head back and closes his eyes. The next few sips taste better than the first few. His stomach is no longer protesting and his head begins to feel light. He takes another gulp before putting the bottle down. His glance meets the miller's, but the bonhomie has disappeared from Heinrich's eyes.

'The other day Karl came home with a bleeding lip. Apparently the doing of your son. Unprovoked, according to Karl.' The miller keeps his expressionless eyes fixed on his worker. 'Now, it's not up to me to judge if it was unprovoked or not. But what is clear is that your son is learning to use his fists at the boxing club in such a way that they can cause harm to others. That needs to stop. I trust you will sort it out.'

Heinrich nearly empties his bottle with the next gulp while he hears Albert say, 'Yes, boss, we understand each other. Of course, I will sort my son out.'

Heinrich's eyes brighten up again. He's regained control of himself and the situation. He winks at Albert while he once again clinks bottles.

'The boy needs to get used to the fact that his father is back.'

And so Albert talked to his son, advising him to stop getting into fights with the local boys otherwise he would be forbidden from continuing boxing at the club. Albert also extracted from the boy the promise that they would go together to the local library to look at some photographic books.

The Warrior Child

THESE IDIOTS. PETER is lying on the top floor of the derelict building. He has a good view from the big opening in the wall without running the risk of being detected himself. If he were to stand up he could even make out the sea from here. No one dares to enter these buildings, and certainly wouldn't attempt to get to the top floor when the staircase is missing and the roof partially gone. But to Peter this floor looks pretty solid.

He turns on to his back and crosses his arms behind his head. Above him the sky displays a beautiful red from the setting sun. Somewhere below he hears Karl and his gang laughing. Soon they won't be laughing any more. When he, Peter, has finished with them. Karl believes that by snitching on Peter to his father, who then straight away talked to Peter's father, who in turn, of course - Peter rolls his eyes - told Peter off for getting into fights, he has stopped Peter. Pah! All it means is that he, Peter, will use more sophisticated war methods. But surrender - never.

More hooting from below travels up to him. He turns back on to his stomach. The bottle and two cigarettes are making the rounds. Karl's gang includes six boys: Karl himself; then Klaus, Dieter, Günther, Gerhard and Erich. They are in Peter's class and the six of them play football in the same team. The gang is feared, especially among the refugee kids, boys and girls alike. Only boys from town who swear to fight all migrants to the death are allowed in. Karl hates everyone from the East because they smell and steal and resemble parasites, he claims. And he says that everyone from the East is lazy and has only come here because they are hoping for an easier life. Peter quickly understood that there's no use contradicting Karl. Even some of the teachers are on his side.

The milksops have closed the bottle. They can't cope with more than a couple of little sips each. And they think they are cool. Any fool can walk into a shop and steal a few cigarettes and a bottle of brandy. And who is interested in that? Only wimps.

Suddenly something hits the back of Peter's head. He ducks. It felt like a stone. He touches his skull. All fine. He must have imagined it.

He places his head down on his forearm. He is more nervous than he thought. Mind you, what he's planning is quite daring. If there is one thing he learned by challenging Karl to a fist fight in order to sort out their situation man to man, it is that the local boys always have the law on their side, regardless of the crimes they commit. But with his action now, Peter will declare war on Karl and his gang. It will be a sign to them that they should watch out, that there is someone observing them, following them, who knows every move they make and could blow their cover.

Crack.

Peter throws himself down again. Damn it. That was certainly a stone that landed there next to him.

'Peter!' A weak voice from the floor below.

He's been discovered. Busted.

'Peter, it's me, Hanne. I know that you're up there.'

Hanne? She's in his class. And plays the piano. Has

116

already spoken to him two or three times. Which means she approached him. He would never have talked to a girl. And she is from here. One has to be careful with them. She might be in cahoots with Karl.

Peter crawls on his forearms to the other side. He peeps carefully over the edge of the floor where the stairs once were.

'Drop down the plank.'

Peter's heart stops. How does she know about the plank?

'Peter, hurry up, before someone sees me here.'

'Are you alone?' He can't see anyone with her, but he prefers to be sure. Up here he is safe – as long as no one comes up. The plank is like a drawbridge. If dropped down, the enemy could take his castle.

'Of course.' Then she adds, 'Please, I'm on your side.'

Hanne needs to disappear from down there as quickly as possible otherwise she will attract attention. And since she clearly isn't willing to leave him alone, he has no other choice than to let her come up. He slowly lowers the plank.

When Peter first devised the plan, he quickly realized that a fresh cowpat or some other animal manure wouldn't have the desired effect. It had to be human faeces. His own.

In the morning, he doesn't go to the loo. After lunch he immediately disappears. He asks his mother for an extra slice of bread and he pinches five plums in Lehmannstrasse. He sits on the beam across the earth closet and eats the plums. Then he waits. But today nothing comes. He pulls up his trousers and runs a few rounds around the camp. Movement always helps. Back on the beam, he aims at the wooden box he has found in the derelict building and hits the target.

He runs as fast as he can because the box smells disgusting.

Luckily no one crosses his path. Hanne glances at the box stony-faced, even though the smell must hit her hard. Peter takes note of her composure in admiration.

'Hello.'

'Hello.'

She follows him silently. He has already explained the plan to her. She even offered to add something of her own to the box, but he declined the offer like a gentleman.

She acts as a lookout while he gets down to work. He fetchs Karl and Co.'s brandy bottle, cigarettes, matches and peppermints out of their hiding place underneath the bushes behind the derelict building. Everything except the bottle is wrapped in old tarpaulin as protection from the damp. Peter fastens a piece of clothes to his face, covering his nose and mouth, before he opens up the tarpaulin and lifts the lid of the box. He pulls a piece of flat wood from his back pocket and begins to smear the shit evenly across the tarpaulin. He rolls it up, making sure that no mark is visible. Then he smears his faeces over the bottle. He only hopes that the smell won't prevent Karl and Co. from reaching blindly into the bushes as they usually do.

But he need not have worried. They roar loudly that something smells disgusting. Of migrants from the East and pigs. But Karl has already knelt down and pulled the tarpaulin out from underneath the bush. And while Gerhard unties the string, Karl has pushed his hand a second time into the undergrowth. The tarpaulin is opened up. On top of the derelict building, Hanne and Peter hold their breath. Karl screams, 'Ergh,' and pulls his hand back from the undergrowth, but he is still gripping the bottle. When he sees what he is holding he screams again. Gerhard jumps up, Karl drops the bottle, staring at his hand in utter disbelief. Everyone moves away from him. For a moment there is silence, until Klaus can be heard saying, 'That is human shit.' Peter and Hanne cover their mouths with their hands in order not to laugh out loud. Karl starts to cry. Big, round tears run down his cheeks. 'I will never be able to get rid of this smell. My dad will be so angry.' For a moment the others look at him in amazement. Their leader is a crybaby. As if by command, they pick up their bikes and speed off, leaving the weeping Karl standing there staring at his hand. He doesn't move for quite a while, sobbing uncontrollably. Peter almost feels sorry for him. But only almost.

Agatha Goes Shopping

IF SHE HAD a handbag she could press it against her stomach to help her walk upright. No. If she had a handbag, it would dangle from her right elbow. Confident.

Agatha enters the swing doors of the department store.

She knows what's happening back in the room. It always smells when she returns from the Saturday market. Their bodily secretions. His body secretions. The longer she stays away, the more chance that the air has cleared. And truth to tell, she's coming to terms with Albert being back. They have found a way of living together, Albert and her: by accepting the inevitable. Mostly they ignore each other, trying to get out of each other's way as much as possible. And just for the record: she never really wanted him dead. God forbid. When she went to the police all those years back, it was to save her daughter and grandson. But anyway, Agatha doesn't want to stir up old stories. And she had better keep her head down because she senses there is trouble brewing between Albert and Peter. The boy is clever. He knows how to handle his father. Promised him not to get into a fist fight again with the local boys, but insisted on continuing with his boxing. Well done!

Today she will stay out even longer. To the left and right, out of the corner of her eye, she notices the clothes rails. Off-the-peg clothing. She never really understood why women – and men – are so keen to buy ready-made clothes. There are only five or six different sizes available. But are there only five or six different bodies? Each body is different. The worst, however, is that the people who buy such clothes don't any longer experience how material can change them, transform them. During the cutting and sewing and fitting, the fabric transforms itself and then transfers its magic on to the person.

There are only a few customers in the department store. Agatha had hoped for more, because then she'd be less noticeable.

Sales assistants are dotted about. Standing around idly, bored. It's inexcusable that they have nothing to do, that they aren't even given a proper task, making themselves useful. But truth to tell, they don't worry her. They can't hold anything against her. Yesterday evening was bathtime. Peter is always allowed to get in first. But this week Agatha came second. The water was still warm. All sweat and dirt dissolved from her skin. She washed her shirt and socks. She smells clean. No one can accuse her of reeking. The young women's eyes follow her. These good-for-nothing sales assistants with their painted nails and painted lips and artificially-coloured hair. But she, Agatha, has the right to be here, just like anyone else.

Agatha has now reached the hat department. She won't stop here.

Her hands itch. The desire to touch beautiful smooth fabric is almost unbearable. She rubs thumb, index and middle finger together. Her fingers are as rough as sandpaper. But clean. She scrubbed them too. Not a single dirt spot remains in the grooves or underneath the nails. If they like, they can check with a magnifying glass. But that of course would never happen. You use a magnifying glass if you can't apprehend something, decipher something. Something exotic that you want to study in more detail. For these people here, these artificially-scented ladies and gentlemen, she's nothing but an old crow, someone they don't want, who came all the way from the East and looks a bit battered after a long flight against the strong winds.

Agatha's jaw pushes forward in defiance.

A crow has feathers.

She fluffs herself up and opens her wings. Their width is more than two metres. Yes, that's right. More than two metres. No one expected that, did they? No one ever expects anything like that from Agatha. Her wings are shiny black and they swish across the rails of ready-made clothes. *Caw. Caw.* She turns her head proudly to the left and to the right.

She directs her glance in front of her. She can now see the fabric department. Huge bolts of material. From this distance it's not yet possible to make out single patterns, or even colours. But soon.

A man appears in front of Agatha. She steps aside, walks around him and stretches her hand forward. Silk. Beautiful, smooth, cold silk.

'Can I help you?'

She closes her eyes, stroking the fabric. She hasn't been near so much beautiful fabric in years. She has to start sewing again. Even if it's only repairs and alterations. In every mended hole, in every widened or tightened skirt, hides the promise of transformation – even if it is only a tiny transformation. Customers come to her with hope. Clothes lead people to believe in better, more beautiful, happier lives. And she, Agatha, is the magician, who can turn all this into reality, by changing the position of a button, by letting out a hem, by repairing the tear in a sleeve. She opens her eyes again.

'I'd like to buy a sewing machine.'

The man's glance wanders from the top of her hair down to the tips of her shoes. But she doesn't budge. Agatha stands her ground.

'What price range are you thinking of?' He pulls his little moustache mockingly upwards.

'I would like some advice.' She's surprised how firm her voice sounds. After all, it's a lie. She can't afford a sewing machine. But one day. 'Are you responsible for the sewing machines?'

For a split second their eyes meet.

'My colleague who is responsible for the sewing machines isn't available at the moment.'

What impertinence. But he won't get off that easily. He can't throw her out; she hasn't caused any problems.

'I will wait till your colleague becomes available. In the meantime, I will look at the fabric.'

Once again she steps around the man. She's summoning her entire strength of mind to pretend that he is not there.

She's standing in the aisle between the tables, suddenly hesitating about which fabric to stroke next, to pay attention to, to rub between her fingers. There are so many. She feels dizzy with choice. Should she head towards the beautiful, delicate, sequined silk, woven with gold and silver thread? Or the cotton – strong in colour, with exciting big patterns, flowers and birds and geometric shapes? Or – in the back – the first warm winter fabrics?

The Kidnapping

H E'S BLINKING INTO the light. They have taken off his blindfold.

'Hit me!' Karl orders Erich. Dieter is holding Karl from behind. 'Hold me tight, Dieter. Tighter. So I don't duck away when Erich hits.' Dieter tightens his grip. Karl is panting heavily. 'Come on! Hit me right in the face.'

Peter is lying on the floor to one side, his hands tied behind his back, his feet tied around the ankles and knees then fastened to his tied hands. They have gagged him so he won't be able to shout for help. Earlier on he had a moment of panic when he thought he couldn't breathe. But then he realized that he can get air through his nose. The gang are standing around him. They seem to be in a cellar somewhere. There's broken glass and debris everywhere. Peter is trying to move. Klaus kicks him in the back at the same time as Erich punches him right in the face. Karl's head flies back, then he lets it hang forward.

'Fuck, man. Not my teeth. Just a black eye.'

Erich stares in horror at Karl. Dieter lets go of him. 'But you said hit hard,' Erich stutters. 'Are you OK?'

Karl jerks up his face with a broad smile. 'Of course! Have I got a black eye?'

Erich leans forward to examine Karl's face. 'Looks good. It's swelling up nicely.'

'Great work, man.' Karl pats Erich on the shoulder. Then

he bends over Peter. 'Look what you've done to me. My dad won't be happy and will give your dad some real, proper shit.'

He brings up some spit from the back of his throat and lets it drop in a big blob on to Peter's face. He then turns away and points with an outstretched arm to the stairs behind Peter's back, and the six boys run off.

Then everything is quiet. Light is falling in through an opening just underneath the ceiling. A kind of window without glass and an iron railing in front of it. Peter lifts his head. Carefully. No, his face didn't fall on any splinters. He's looking over his shoulder. The door stands open. Beyond it are dark, narrow stairs covered in glass. Using his foot, Peter pivots round to see better. Yes, he knows where he is. In the cellar of the derelict building behind which Karl and his gang always meet. At the bottom of a cul-de-sac.

No one will find him here unless they tell someone. And they won't.

Peter tries to wiggle his hands, his feet. They knew what they were doing. These are proper knots and they used a proper rope. For a moment he feels defeated. He will never get out of here. And he doubts they will come back. Boys like Karl are always good at forgetting their crimes the moment they commit them. So that when they plead innocent they really believe in their own righteousness. Peter has come across this type before.

They waited for him in Ziegelhofweg. Someone jumped on his back, so quickly he didn't have time to react. They pulled him into the ditch, many arms and legs, he had no chance. They gagged him with a small towel. Peter tried his best to fight, throwing himself from side to side. Then all of a sudden everything around him disappeared.

He swallows with difficulty. Yes, he remembers now, someone sat on his chest and pushed a knee into his throat. When he regained consciousness, it was dark. There was a rattling underneath him. He was lying on his side, tied up, blindfolded. A blanket covering him.

Oddly, in that moment, he wasn't scared. He didn't have time. His brain was too busy understanding where he was. He realized quickly that he was being transported in a handcart. He was strapped down. The cart moved fast. His brain logged the information. In the meantime, his body was very still, attempting to minimize the impact.

The journey didn't take long. When they stopped, they carried him and placed him down on the concrete floor.

'If you say just one word to anyone, we will kill you.' Karl was kneeling beside him, his spit dripping down Peter's cheek as he untied the blindfold.

Karl's spit on Peter's cheek has now dried. Peter is tensing his body, trying to scream, to shout, to produce some sort of sound. Trying to move, to shift, to do anything. He feels his hands, his ankles scraping across pieces of glass. Exhausted, he rests his head on the only spot that seems to be free of broken glass.

What if he never gets out of here? No, no, he will. They will come back for him. Once Karl has run home and told his story about the black eye, they will check on him. They won't let him die here. They are show-offs, that's all, talking the talk. But they would never actually let anyone die. No one lets anyone die willingly. You only kill when you are being attacked. And he didn't attack Karl and his gang. Well . . . only a bit. Not really. He just let them put their hands into his shit. That's all he's done.

He watches the sunlight move across the floor. Then he watches it retreat. Then he watches it being pulled back through the opening within seconds. Gone.

It will be some time before his mother and grandmother become worried. His mouth is hurting. His tongue is dry in his throat. Cold is creeping into his body from underneath.

A bird is chirping loudly outside the window. It's a very shrill sound. Not beautiful at all. Not like birds are supposed to sound.

Suddenly a foot appears in Peter's field of vision at the top of the stairs. Pushing forward tentatively. A red sock in a sandal. Then another foot. Then a head bending forward almost down to the feet to see what's down there. Two pigtails touching the shoes. Immediately the head disappears again and Hanne comes racing down the stairs.

She frees him from his bondage and they sit down at the bottom of the stairs. He is rubbing his wrists. Hanne's knee is bleeding from where she bent down to untie him.

'There's a piece of glass in your knee. Can I pull it out?' His voice sounds hoarse. Quite manly, he thinks. And that makes him feel better, hoping that his new voice will stay for a while.

She nods and he bends over her knee, pulls the glass out, holding it proudly between index finger and thumb, wanting to bring it closer to her eyes to show her.

'Don't.' Hanne squeezes her eyes tightly together.

Girls! He throws it away.

They emerge from the building cautiously, looking left and right, in front and behind, to make sure that they don't walk straight into the arms of Karl and his gang.

'I don't think they will come,' Hanne says.

They race out of the cul-de-sac and run all the way to Hanne's street, where they stop to catch their breath. Hanne has to be home in five minutes.

'How did you know I was there?'

'I didn't. It was pure chance. Because I wanted to see you, so I came to the only place I thought you might be.'

For a fleeting moment Peter feels he ought to say something funny right now. To make a joke. To lighten the atmosphere. Because what she has just said is so nice, he almost can't believe it. But then he looks at Hanne and she obviously meant it just the way she said it. From her stern expression it's clear she found nothing odd in her statement.

She stops walking. Her house is the next one.

She briefly puts her hand on his chest, then turns and runs off.

'I'll see you tomorrow at school,' she calls back over her shoulder, waving her right hand in the air.

Peter has to admit he's never met a nicer girl. He watches her disappear into her front garden, then he turns and starts walking back to the camp, every now and again kicking a stone in front of him. He's really quite confused. In the last few hours he's experienced the most horrible thing ever and the nicest thing ever. Is that how life works? He sighs. He doesn't have time to ponder this question now. He needs to head back home and explain everything to his parents, his father in particular. Peter is sure his dad will understand. And now he might even realize how mean and horrible Karl is.

He lifts his head and sees his father turn into the camp on his bike. Peter breaks into a trot.

The Trophy

ALBERT IS RED in the face as he tears open the door, storms in and sits down on the bed. Without taking off his boots or washing himself. Which he usually does. His routine. To which he sticks without fail. But not today.

'Where is the boy?'

Agatha picks up the torn jumper she has started to unravel in order to knit a new one, and is about to leave. She has learned to be out of the room when Albert comes home. He's ten minutes earlier than usual. He is panting. He must have rushed.

She is already halfway across the room.

'You stay here! No one is leaving this room.'

Albert has not raised his head or his voice, but the tone makes Agatha freeze in mid-stride. For a moment she struggles with herself. Instinctively she wants to walk on, to defy him. How dare he order her about like that? Something, however, tells her that his anger is not directed at her. Yet. But if she continues it might very well be, distracting him from the actual cause.

Albert now lifts his head and looks straight at his wife.

'I asked where the boy is.'

Trude stands by the table. She had started to clear it in readiness for supper.

'He should be back any moment,' she says. 'You're early today. Let me get you a footbath,' she continues, and turns to fetch the big bowl, with the idea of heading to the kitchen shack and boiling some water.

'No!' Albert jumps up. 'You will also stay here.'

No one is to leave the room. This situation has to be sorted once and for all. He's turning into a laughing stock in the eyes of the miller. Yesterday when the miller said to him, 'I take it you've spoken to your son?' Albert confirmed that he had. After all, he had struck a deal with his son. No more getting into fights with the local boys, and by accompanying his father on some photographic excursions, —he can continue boxing in the club. And this morning he said to the miller, 'Peter is getting interested in photography. He's calming down. The last years have been tough on the boy, but now everything is getting back to normal.' He trusted Peter to stick to the deal. More fool him!

Albert had been getting on his bike when the miller came out of the office waving at him to wait. 'My wife just telephoned me in tears. Karl has come home with a swollen eye. Peter apparently went berserk.' For a moment, all Albert could do was look at the miller's moving lips. The words arrived afterwards, although his body had already understood. Blood was rushing in his ears. The boy had not obeyed him. But even worse, it meant he did not stick to deals, to commitments. The miller might have said something else. Albert doesn't know. He mumbled, 'I will sort it out,' got on his bike and pedalled home as hard as he could, relieved that he had that distance between him and his son.

And he wants Trude and Agatha to be here so no one will

think of undermining him again or going behind his back. Ever again.

Peter opens the door. He knows, the boy thinks. He can tell from his father's eyes, the way he stands there, the way he stares at him. His mother, too, has turned to look at him. Only Agatha hasn't lifted her gaze, hasn't stopped doing what she is doing there in the corner.

'I—' Peter starts.

'Close the door!' Albert shouts.

Peter closes the door.

'Come here!' Albert points with his right index finger at a spot in front of him.

Peter obeys.

Agatha continues unravelling the jumper and winding the yarn into a ball. She's working fast but with great concentration, changing direction frequently as she winds, making sure that the wool doesn't get tangled into knots. It's quite worn already, and if she had to pull hard to undo a knot the yarn might break. And that'd be a pity.

She feels sorry for Peter – and for Trude. This man has been bad news from the beginning. Oh yes, he has. He has never been taught how to behave. And how could he? He's from the gutter. Nowadays he might no longer be womanizing, but his temper is getting worse. Self-control is something he has never learned. But Agatha knows that if she interferes she would lessen the impact of Albert's behaviour. Detract from it. And although there is nothing more she has dedicated her life to than protecting Trude and Peter, in this very moment she feels it is necessary for both of them to see Albert's true nature. Especially Trude, who is still convinced that Albert was the right choice. The only thing guaranteed to sway her would be if she thought that he posed a risk to Peter, behaving in such an irresponsible way as to harm the boy. Like during the war, listening to the Black Radio. Agatha is convinced that her daughter knows that it was her mother who went to the police. Maybe she didn't want to admit it to herself at the time. But surely by now? And also Trude must have known deep down, in her gut, and approved that her mother had acted to protect her daughter's life, and Peter's, from the consequences of Albert's thoughtless behaviour. Underneath, Trude knew the danger Albert posed to his own son.

The only thing Agatha now has to do is to keep quiet and unravel the jumper without tangling the yarn.

'I can explain,' Peter starts again.

'Be quiet!' Albert cuts him short.

Peter throws an imploring glance towards his mother, who almost imperceptibly shakes her head, begging him with her eyes not to speak. It's bound to make things worse.Albert points to the trophy on the shelf.

'Fetch that for me, Peter.'

Peter hasn't moved, isn't moving. Something bad is about to happen, he can sense it. His eyes are fixed on the golden boxer. He has to save his trophy from this man. The trophy doesn't even belong to him. It's only on loan until next year. He shuffles towards the shelf very slowly so he has more time to think. But he can't think. He has reached the shelf, lifts his arm. Very, very slowly. The father is standing to his left. The door is to the right. If he's quick enough he might be able to seize the trophy and run to the door . . .

'You are going nowhere.'

Albert grabs hold of Peter's right hand, which is on the trophy. The boy is not as smart as he thinks. Albert is not going to be outwitted by his own son.

'Give it to me.'

Peter shakes his head.

'Let go.'

Peter again shakes his head.

'Albert, please.' Trude's voice.

Albert lifts his hand from Peter's and takes a step back towards the door, keeping his son in full view.

Peter hasn't turned around.

'Dad, please,' he begs. Why isn't his grandmother helping him? Why is she just sitting there, not even looking up?

'Give it to your mother.' Albert points with a dismissive movement of his head towards Trude.

'Dad, please. I can explain. I . . . Karl . . .'

'Do not provoke me even more.' Albert's voice is shaking now.

'Mum, please do something! This isn't my trophy.'

Trude takes hold of Peter's wrist. 'Shh,' she whispers. 'Give it to me.'

'Don't give it to him, Mum, don't!' Peter lifts the trophy off the shelf. 'They won't let me fight in the club if he does anything to the trophy.'

'Let go, Peter.'

Trude takes the golden boxer from him, but at the last moment Peter changes his mind.

'No, I can't.' He's reaching his hand out again.

'Don't you dare, boy.' His father.

'It's OK, Peter.' Trude smiles at her son. 'Don't worry. I will look after it.'

'Hand it to me, Trude,' Albert says.

If she hands him the trophy he will smash it. Peter's shining treasure has been a thorn in Albert's side since the beginning. As if that is the only thing that has happened since he was away, and he can't bear it.

Out of the corner of her eye Trude becomes aware of a tiny movement. Peter's hand. It is shaking. Like an old man's hand. Trude looks down at the object she is holding. The sight of her son's shaking hand is too much. She wants to protect that hand. She wants to preserve for her son what makes him happy. She has protected him from so much evil and harm over the years. Why is she hesitating now? How can she even contemplate not defending him, his trophy, his boxing? She knows how much it matters to him. If there is one person in this room who could succeed in walking out with the trophy unharmed, one person who could stand between Albert and his rage, then it is her, Trude.

She now cradles the little boxer statue in her arms like a baby.

Without shifting her head, Trude's eyes wander to her mother. She knows what her mother is thinking, can feel it in every part of her body. That Albert's true nature is becoming apparent. That Albert's behaviour is unacceptable. That Albert's behaviour has always been unacceptable, irresponsible. That he doesn't understand his own son, can't see how important boxing is for the boy. That Albert is doing harm to Peter. That he always only thinks about himself. That it is Trude's duty to protect her son. That it is time for her to realize that Albert was a bad choice. From the beginning.

But Albert was never a bad choice for her. Not from the beginning and not now. He has come back for her from the war, where her mother sent him, hoping he would perish and never return. Just because Trude's father went to war. He came back, too, it's true. With three missing toes and a wound in his chest. And the wound never healed. Of course, a mother should always want the best for her daughter. That's a fairy tale, though. Life is more complicated.

Trude shakes her head imperceptibly. Her mother is not a bad woman. But nor is Albert. Albert was not a bad choice. And he is not a bad father to Peter. If she wants the old Albert back, she needs to let the returning Albert express his rage. Even if it hurts Peter. But there will be ways forward. Afterwards.

She turns to face Albert and locks her eyes on to his. She hands him the trophy.

For a moment no one moves. Even Agatha has stopped winding the yarn.

Then Albert lifts the trophy and smashes it down on the table.

Hanne's Plan

PETER IS RUNNING so fast that his chest hurts, his legs hurt, his throat hurts. And that's fine. He wants everything to cause him pain so he doesn't need to feel the biggest hurt of all: his hatred for his father. Why did he come back? He hates him so much, like nothing else in life. What do you do when you hate someone so much?

He throws a stone against Hanne's window. The curtain is already drawn.

He throws another stone but keeps a close eye on the window below, which is the front room. The curtains there are drawn too. Suddenly he freezes, ashamed. What is he doing, going begging a girl for comfort and sympathy?

He's about to turn away when the curtain upstairs moves and Hanne's silhouette appears in the window. In the very same moment he notices the curtain downstairs moving too. He ducks, crouching against the wall beneath the window, because if he were discovered by Hanne's parents they would take him back to his place. To his father. The man he never wants to see again. Ever. In his entire life.

'He smashed my trophy.'

As he was crouching against the wall, wondering if Hanne had seen him, the upper window opened and a torch with a note attached to it landed on the grass in front of him. He should wait for her upstairs in the derelict building, the note said. But she couldn't leave before her parents had gone to bed, so they wouldn't notice. He approached the building with a pounding heart, torch in one hand, big stick in the other. Once he had reached the top floor and had pulled up the plank he felt safer. He sat in a corner and watched the stars appear one after another. He would persuade Hanne to run away with him. He wanted so badly to run away, run away from his father.

'I can't leave my mum alone with him.'

He is sobbing now. Although he had sworn to himself that he wouldn't cry in front of Hanne.

'But my mum won't go. My grandma, yes, she would. I don't think she likes my father either.'

Hanne's sitting very close to him. Their shoulders and arms are touching. It's very dark now. The stars have disappeared behind clouds and that is good, because Peter is shivering and sobbing, and snot and tears are running down his face.

He tries, tries very hard to get hold of himself. His arms around his legs, he's pressing his knees against his chest. He has to become tough. Toughen up. Why isn't he tough? Crying in front of a girl. The only person he knows here – a girl. The only person who seems to like him here – a girl. In this stupid, godforsaken place.

He feels her hand on his shoulder.

He doesn't like what's happening inside him now. There is a darkness, an empty darkness spreading through him. The darkness inside and outside are becoming one. He's dissolving. In a moment he will have gone. Disappeared. But he doesn't want to disappear. He just wants to get away from his father. His father? This man! This is not his father. How can it be his father? Just because his mother says it's his father! He doesn't need a father. He was doing fine without this father. Everyone was doing fine. No. No. No. He is not going to dissolve because of this man. This Albert. He just needs to find a way of never seeing him again.

'Can I put my head on your shoulder?' he hears himself asking. And he immediately hates himself for it, but the words are out. He can't take them back, especially because Hanne is already saying, 'Yes.'

No, he won't. He won't. He won't. He won't. He grabs his right hand with his left and squeezes them both together in an attempt to prevent himself from moving any other body part, including his head. The pain in his hand is so great, it's spreading through his entire body. And it's covering up the big black hole inside him. Then suddenly he feels something soft. Hanne's arms around him. Her cheek against his shoulder. They sit like this for a long time. And that's OK. It's very dark here and no one needs to know. Eventually he releases his hands.

Peter stalls. At the end of the road he sees pupils crowding into the school. He's clutching his schoolbooks tight to his chest. He promised Hanne. He shakes his head. He has fulfilled the first part of the promise, but he can't do this. He turns round.

He forces himself not to run, walking briskly, looking down. There are still children heading in the opposite direction towards school. Hopefully no one will recognize him. He halts again. Where should he go? He can't go home and he doesn't want to go back to the derelict house. Someone bumps into him. Frightened, he jumps to the side.

'Look out!'

A little kid half his size smiles at him and continues running towards school. Peter presses his body against the wooden fence. He can't face Karl and his gang. Impossible. It was all Hanne's idea. He wanted to run away.

'Where to?' Hanne asked.

'I don't know. But I want to run away. Will you come with me?'

For a moment Hanne was very quiet. Then she said, 'No,' into the darkness and took her arm from his shoulder, moving a few centimetres away.

'Why not?'

'Because we're children,' she replied matter-of-factly. And she sounded so grown up and he suddenly didn't like her at all.

'Then I'll go on my own,' he replied defiantly.

'OK, then, go.'

He couldn't see, but he realized that she had got up and was moving the plank.

'No, wait.' He didn't want to be alone. He really did not want to be alone.

'What?' She was crouching by the other side, ready to lower the plank.

'I don't want to go on my own.'

'Then stay here.'

She was still holding the plank and for a short while all he could hear was her breathing and his own.

'Can you sit next to me again?' he asked eventually.

She put the plank down and sat close to him, their thighs touching.

'What shall I do?'

'You need to go back home.'

'And my father?'

She shrugged. He could feel it. 'That's what fathers are like.'

'Your father too?'

'Sometimes.'

Again, silence.

'And my trophy? They will expel me from the boxing club if they find out.'

'You don't have to return it for another ten months, do you? By then we will have figured something out.'

Peter began to feel much warmer inside.

'I've thought about something else,' she then said. 'If I were you, I'd go to school tomorrow as if nothing had happened. You don't say anything to your parents about Karl and his gang tying you up. You don't say anything to the teachers. You don't say anything to Karl or his friends. You walk past them as if nothing has happened. And if they try to provoke you into another fight, you walk away. And—' Hanne pauses for a moment '—you apologize to your father for hitting Karl again.'

'No! Not that. I won't apologize for something I didn't do.'

Peter pushes himself away from the fence. Of course he can walk into school as if nothing had happened. Why did he suddenly panic? Wasn't last night much harder? As he returned, his mother was sitting on a rock by the entrance of the camp, waiting for him. When she saw him she jumped up and wanted to take him in her arms, but he backed away.

'I'm not going to share the bed with Dad any longer.'

He had left Hanne's a while before and walked the empty night streets, thinking of ways to punish his father. He wanted to make him suffer big-time, but the only thing he could come up with was that he wouldn't share his bed any longer. It was pathetic, but that was all he could think of. His father would have to squeeze in with his mother or grandmother. Peter didn't care which.

'You'll have to share a bed with Grandma, then,' his mother said.

Peter shrugged. That was fine by him.

He's now walking slowly, very slowly towards school. He hears the first bell. In five minutes the second bell will ring. He's the only one left on the pavement. He will be late and he will be sent to the headmaster's office. Still, that's a small price to pay for the pleasure of knowing that right now Karl's eyes are on Peter's empty seat. They might have been back to the derelict building in the morning and found him gone. Or they might not and now begin to worry that they have left him there to die. He will be on Karl's mind, one way or another. And it won't be an easy feeling. So he wants Karl to sit with that uneasy feeling a bit longer. He reaches the school gate just in time as the caretaker is locking up.

'Very late this morning, young man.'

Peter smiles. Being late for school no longer stresses him out. What he's experienced over the last twelve hours is far more important than school. He's encountered real life. And it made a man of him. Peter is about to lift his hand and tap his hat, like an American actor who plays a gangster with a good heart. Only at the last moment does he refrain. It might irritate the caretaker and he doesn't want to do that. He has set his sights on bigger things now.

For a couple of minutes he stands outside the classroom. He's never been in the corridor on his own before, and there's an eerie atmosphere: not so much quietness, but a sense of absence, as if school corridors are meant to be filled with noise – screaming and running and laughter. From inside the classroom he doesn't hear anything either. He presses his ear closer to the wood. Maybe there is no one here? Maybe they are all dead? He shakes his head. What a stupid idea. He's seen children hurrying to school. He can also detect a faint murmur from other classrooms.

'Sit down!'

Herr Schulze, the maths teacher. He didn't think about that. Herr Schulze is the strictest teacher in almost the entire school. Only Herr von der Weide, the natural sciences teacher, is worse. With him you try not even to breathe. Herr von der Weide hates loud breathing, can't stand it. And sometimes the entire class has to hold its breath for three minutes or four. One of the girls fainted. Herr von der Weide can't believe his bad luck to belong to a nation of weaklings and losers. He fought for the Kaiser and those were the days. Of real heroes. Of courage. Of pride. Herr Schulze too thinks that all he is left to teach is *Weicheier*, sissies. And he often tells the story of Adolf Bauer, the last great boy worth teaching, according to Herr Schulze, who aged eleven defended Hamburg against the enemy until the last moment and died a heroic death on 1 May 1945. Afterwards the class has to stand in silence in memory of Adolf Bauer, upright with hands held behind their back.

Carefully Peter places a hand on the door handle. He shouldn't delay his entry any longer. With each moment that passes Herr Schulze is bound to increase the number of ruler strokes to his palm. He pushes down the handle and opens the door just wide enough to slip through. The class is looking straight ahead towards the teacher's desk. Herr Schulze has stood up and is turning to face the blackboard when his eye catches Peter standing in the doorway. He halts. As if on command, everyone turns to look at the door. Peter freezes. Then he steps inside and pulls the door shut. He keeps his gaze on the teacher.

'I'm sorry for coming late, Herr Schulze. My grandmother fell ill this morning.'

He's ready to stride up to the teacher's desk, to put his hand out, to receive his punishment.

'Sit down,' Herr Schulze says, nodding in the vague direction of Peter's place at the back of the class.

Peter hesitates. Is the teacher serious? But Herr Schulze has already started to write equations on the blackboard. Peter passes Karl and Klaus and Dieter and Günther and Gerhard and Erich. They don't dare to move even their heads, because they are scared of Herr Schulze who, despite having turned his back towards the class, is capable of detecting the slightest shift on a seat – 'Don't forget, I was a sapper. Sappers are the first to arrive in enemy territory and our lives and the lives of our troops depend on us detecting the smallest movement or noise. And never did any one of our men die because of me.' But Peter feels the eyes of the boys on him. As he puts one foot in front of the other, he wonders if he can sense what their glances mean. Admiration? Fear? Surprise? Frustration? Anger? As he takes the last couple of steps he suddenly realizes that he doesn't actually care what these boys think or feel. He lifts his head and looks over to Hanne.

Albert's Dream

A S LONG AS you can keep disorder at bay you have control. You can see clearly, you know what step to take next. Albert can't stand chaos. He used to be able to tolerate it. In fact, when he was young he never made a distinction between order and disorder. Never thought about it. That wasn't how he perceived the world, neatly divided into two camps, with judgements attached: good or bad. But now he's convinced, has become convinced over the last years, that chaos is the enemy of the people. Every now and again, for a brief moment, he looks longingly back to a time when he wasn't so clear-sighted. He knows that this lack of a clear view helped him to take good photographs. He was open to surprise, to being surprised. But then again, there is no need to shed tears over this loss.

He looks at the flour bags. Everyone has gone home, the miller too. And he should also leave; it's not his business to sort out the flour bags now. The miller is happy to leave them where they were dropped earlier. But they are far too close to the entrance of the barn. Albert was in the office today, helping with the accounts. If he had been here when they were brought in he would have made sure that they were neatly stacked towards the back of the barn, where it's drier. Here at the front, if the wind blows at a certain angle, rain could come in underneath the door. Or the door could blow open altogether. The weather looks good. No rain or storm is forecast. But you never know, do you?

Albert walks out of the barn. Closes its door, pushes the bolt in front of it. Fastens the big key chain. The miller has now given him keys to the office and the barn. A responsibility. He shouldn't have looked in here.

His boss had checked everything. Albert saw him through the office window, walking into the barn and then locking up. So what is he doing here? He came here to fetch his bike, which he left behind the barn. He should fetch his bike and cycle home.

'Happy birthday,' Trude had whispered into his ear in the morning. And: 'I have a surprise for you tonight.'

It's been a busy day. He's had numbers in front of him all day. Lucky him. He lost himself in them. Numbers are beautiful. They don't allow disorder. If the rules of logic are not obeyed or broken, numbers shriek and complain an awful lot. And then you sort things out and they are quiet. And inside you a beautiful calm feeling of order and a sense of control arise.

He walks around the barn to the back.

They receive 200 grams of bread, 5 grams of butter and 200 grams of millet in the morning. At lunchtime another 200 grams of bread and 150 grams of millet and in the evening 200 grams of millet and 5 grams of butter. They should have received 150 grams of millet a day more, spread over the three meals, but he'd worked out that it was missing from each person's meal and made up for by pouring more water into the soup. Knowing the shortcomings in mathematical terms did not fill his stomach, but he could hold on to the figures. They could not trick him. Not him.

But they did.

He's now standing in front of his bicycle. He bends down and rolls up his right trouser leg.

This is all in the past. He's a lucky man. He's alive. He has a family. His family is doing well. Peter is getting on with the other boys, becoming a decent lad. He's doing well at school, too. Not like Albert, who dropped out of school at Peter's age. Had to drop out to earn money for himself and his sick mother. No, Peter will have a different life. He will finish school and go to university and then he can make a living wherever he wants in the world. Maybe even in America. And next spring, hopefully, they will be able to move into one of the new flats that are being built right this very moment. And then Peter will have his own desk to study at. Albert will buy him a desk. He's saving up for it.

He pushes the bike to the front. There is something rattling at the barn door. He stops. Listens. No. Can't have been. There is no wind. Nothing. He's looking up into the clear, early evening sky. Mist is settling in. The air carries a fresh bite. He takes a deep breath, fills his lungs. He's going to enjoy the ride home. His lifts his right leg over the saddle. There it is again, the rattling. The barn door is rattling. He pulls his leg back, lays down the bike. As he straightens up again, he sees a shadow flitting across the side of the building.

It's very dark, except for a couple of dim gaslights at the edge of the area he's been allocated. He is raking. He thinks there are others working in adjacent areas, but he can't be sure. He likes the thought. He can't be the only one. Although he's never seen anyone else, no other prisoner. Two guards bring him here in a vehicle. They hand him the rake. While he rakes, they take turns sleeping inside the vehicle. Sometimes they switch on the lights and sometimes he can hear the radio faintly. There's no moon. There's never been a moon since he started working here. Every now and then they don't fetch him for a night. He likes to think that these are the moon nights and that they are being kind to him. The raking is better in the dark.

They picked him out at evening call and told him to come to the overseer's barracks.

'Happy birthday. Do you want an extra bowl of soup?' the officer behind the desk asked. He said yes straight away. He didn't think about the others, and that it'd be unfair to them if he got more. He didn't ask either what he needed to do for it. Or why he had been chosen. He just wanted that extra bowl of soup. He thought he was lucky. Perhaps they chose him because he was still stronger than others who had been in this camp for longer.

No one knows that he receives an extra bowl of soup. He hasn't told anyone. He decided on that the first evening he was fetched. He sat in the vehicle and didn't know where he was going. The guards seemed friendly, they offered him a cigarette. And he thought he shouldn't tell anyone about the extra bowl of soup or the cigarette. He didn't want to attract envy.

When he was on his way back to camp that night, he still thought he shouldn't tell anyone. But this time because of the work he was doing: no one would have agreed to do this, even for two bowls of soup. What if he had said no? They all think he has to work the extra hours at night as punishment. Six hours for an extra bowl of soup, which means he only gets two hours of sleep a night. But those two hours he spends in a deep sleep because he has a bowl of soup in his stomach. The others think he sleeps because he is exhausted. The first couple

148

of nights he too thought that. Until he realized that he could sleep because he has that extra bowl of soup. Of course it isn't enough to satisfy his hunger. But it's an extra 200 grams of millet. No butter, mind. Their evening meal consists of 200 grams of millet and 5 grams of butter. And then he sleeps for two dreamless hours. They are the best dreamless hours he's ever enjoyed. Yes, enjoyed. He needs to enjoy them. Because once the night work stops he will never again sleep for two dreamless hours. He will be raking all night long. There is a lot to rake. He receives the bowl straight after his shift from the guard to whom he hands back the rake.

Sometimes it rains. That's the worst. Because then the raking doesn't go well and he has to get down on his hands and knees and use his fingers. The white bones in his hands. And suddenly they are shiny, like glittering stars. There are men and women and children. Lots of children. So many children. Sometimes they are still wrapped in shreds of clothes. Often they are not. His job is to rake everything into a big heap at the edge of the field. The earth has to be smooth, ready for grass to be planted, flowers to bloom, trees to take root, houses to be built. When he arrives the next night, yesterday's heap has always disappeared and he's given a new area. He doesn't understand where all these corpses come from. There are thousands and thousands and thousands of them.

After a few days, perhaps five, he wants to stop. He doesn't care about the extra bowl of soup any longer. He just doesn't want to go back. When they come to fetch him, he refuses to get up from his bunk. They ram the rifle butt into his stomach, then drag him outside and into the vehicle. He faints on the way and wakes up staring into the empty eye sockets of a tiny skull. The rake is lying on top of him. He continues to rake and concentrates on the soup and the two hours of dreamless sleep. He doesn't know how long the raking will go on for. Days or weeks or months. Eventually they stop fetching him. First one night, then two nights, then three nights. The raking, of course, continues. Every night he is busy raking. And during the day. When he's idle. Lazing about. Running the danger of letting things fall into disarray. Then he has to rake too. And there are so many fields. And it never stops.

Trude looks at the table. It's a proper birthday table. Around Albert's plate she has placed a daisy chain. In the middle stands a glass with three red asters. She borrowed two proper wine glasses from her boss at work, who also provided her with four red candles – those, of course, against payment. Trude fixes the candles onto the table with dripping wax. She lights them. It's now nearly dark. She sent Agatha and Peter to the double-bill at the cinema; Hanne's parents allowed the girl to join them for the first showing. Albert should be home any moment. Trude expected him even earlier. But then again, it might be nice if he walks into the candlelit room. She has opened a bottle of wine. The pot of meat, potatoes and red cabbage is keeping warm under the blanket. She's washed her hair and, having worn it in four little buns all afternoon, it now falls in beautiful waves on to her shoulders. It's getting thicker again. She picks up the wine bottle and for a moment ponders if she should pour some into the glasses. No. It looks more impressive and glamorous to have a full bottle on the table. She decides to leave the candles burning. It would be a pity if Albert were to come in and the candles weren't lit. She walks over to the bed and puts her hand underneath the blanket. Yes, the food is still warm. She goes to the door and opens it. She closes the door again and sits down at the table.

She's been here before. Waiting for Albert.

It's heavy. Too heavy for him really. He's squatting, pulling the next sack with both arms over his head and on to his back. What's he talking about? Too heavy for him? He's already done ten, only ten more to go. The first sack he tried to push and pull across the floor. But he shouldn't have, it started ripping. He can pull them a bit. Into this corner so he can help himself getting up. He's now pushing the sack hard into the corner to create resistance that makes it easier for him to stand up. He's panting hard. But he's coming up. He's straight. Now the hardest bit, moving away from the wall. That's when he risks losing his balance most. He shuffles a couple of steps forward. Sways. Then he is still. He starts walking, one step at a time, bending forward but not too much. Spit is dripping from his mouth. The saliva is dark. Dark as blood. He ignores it. It's pretty dark all around him. He stops, trying to catch his breath. He feels his arms being pulled further and further backwards. He has to keep on going, he's nearly there. No rest. Rests are dangerous. They unbalance. He has to get back into the moving rhythm. Forward. Number eleven, he is carrying number eleven. Afterwards will be number twelve. Or number nine, counting backwards. Nine, eight, seven, six . . . He collapses. He feels how his hands let go of the sack in slow motion. He'd love to prevent it from happening, but he can't do anything about it. He slams down. The sack is tearing, spraying white flour everywhere.

Trude can see a dim light coming through the open barn door. She bends deeper over the handlebars. As she was waiting she suddenly remembered how as a little girl her mother was gone one morning and she tried to get to her but couldn't. Someone or something prevented her. But she fought to help her mother. So why was she now sitting here waiting, waiting doing nothing? She's no longer a little girl. She's now longer trapped in a place she can't get out of.

She knocked on Gerda's door and borrowed her bike.

Something has happened to Albert. She feels it in her stomach. She is pedalling hard.

Albert's bike is lying in front of the barn. Trude jumps off her bike.

There is Albert in the middle of the floor. Not moving.

Something soft behind his back.

'Albert.' Trude's voice. A hand strokes his brow. Trude's hand.

He used to own a photograph. It showed Trude in a light summer dress, smiling into the camera, one hand raised to her forehead to shield her eyes from the sun. Behind her a meadow of buttercups. They made love in the meadow that day.

The photograph was eventually taken away from him. And her beautiful face, the face he had fallen in love with, faded. At first he didn't notice that he was no longer able to recall it, because for a while he still saw the buttercups. Bright yellow. None of the men really talked about women. Maybe at the beginning. Some of them might have mentioned fiancées, wives, women they knew. The very young ones, the sixteen- and seventeen-year-olds, often screamed for their mothers in their sleep. But they were also the ones who died quickly, the young ones. Hunger devoured everything. They talked about food. And colours. That's how Albert knew that he could still remember the yellow buttercups. But eventually they too disappeared. Years ago.

'Albert.'

He feels an arm around his waist. He is lying on his side. Then he begins to understand where he is.

The Doll

A S FAR AS Agatha is concerned, her daughter has decided to side with her husband against her mother. Agatha shrugs. Well, so be it. Agatha has tried her best. No one can accuse her of being a bad mother. Eventually children have to learn to stand on their own two feet and be allowed to make mistakes. Agatha sighs. Then she straightens up. This is no time to be idle.

She rings the doorbell.

'*Guten Tag.* I'd like to offer my services as a seamstress.'

'Thank you, but there is nothing we need doing at the moment.'

And the door would be shut on her. She's been through these scenarios in her head many times. Agatha is not deluded, she has a split second to convince her potential customer of the magic her hands are capable of performing when they get in contact with needles and thread and fabric.

She looks to the left and right. It's a delightful area. Beautiful two-storey houses, each with their own garden. They must have been built not long before the war. No bombs fell here. In the window next to the door sits a black cat. It's a cold, frosty morning with a light fog in the air.

It didn't take her long to figure out which sales assistants to avoid. And she is especially careful when the ghastly manager is on duty. But some sales assistants don't mind her spending time in their department, in particular the ones who look vacant and spend hours examining themselves in the mirror. The more make-up and the redder their lips and nails, the less they are disturbed by Agatha's presence. Because they don't care and because they don't see her. Agatha also quickly became aware of returning customers, women dressed decently in hats and coats, handbags and gloves. They would hold this or that fabric up against themselves, looking into the mirror, turning left and right and sometimes even whirling around, their eyes twinkling, their lips pouting or smiling seductively or teasingly or naughtily. These women are not young, in their forties and fifties. The really young ones buy off the peg. But the older women know how to dream. They remember the good times. The young ones have no memory.

Agatha hears movement inside the house. The cat strokes its whiskers as if waving to her, then jumps off the windowsill and disappears.

Eventually these women have to put the fabric back on the table. Sometimes they stare at the price tag and Agatha observes them making calculations in their heads. How many metres they need, how many hours of labour this or that dress or costume would require. And then the big question: would it be worth the money in the end? Would they look into the mirror, transformed, not recognizing themselves? Again and again Agatha has been overcome by the desire to walk up to one of these women and whisper into her ear, 'I can make it happen for you. I can work magic with my hands.' And then she watches them walking over to the patterns, leafing through them, contemplating, holding a pattern against a fabric, nodding approvingly or turning up their noses. These women know what they want, they know what works, they are no one's fool. But they don't know how to get it.

The door opens.

'Herr Lemke?' Agatha smiles tentatively.

That too she has practised. And she has observed the manager in the department store, seen how he behaves with customers he feels are likely to spend money. Agatha has left nothing to chance. It's a one-shot opportunity. She had better succeed. Peter's trophy needs to be replaced. If the boxing club finds out they might expel him. That must not happen. For Peter's sake. But also because then Albert would have got his way.

'Yes?' Herr Lemke's expression is cautious but not unfriendly.

She's seen him twice before from afar, once walking along the road beside his wife and once through the lit window in the evening. Up close he's exactly what she expected: mid-forties, tall, strongly built. His dark blond hair swept back with shiny grease. Today, on his day off, he's wearing a black polo neck and grey trousers. She allows herself a quick glance at his hands. Smaller than one would expect for such a big man, but just what she assumed for an amateur violin player and music lover.

'Frau Lemke!'

Agatha was stroking the coral and gold floral silk that had only recently come in.

'How do you do? And how is your husband? Is he playing again? His Vivaldi was so divine.'

The two women were standing only a few metres away from her. Agatha moved on to the next bolt of fabric, closer to them.

'Oh, you know, Frau Krüger, my husband will never be the same again since Kurt died. He had such high hopes for our eldest. Karl just isn't the same. Still, the other day he picked up the violin again. He hadn't played since Kurt was killed.'

Agatha kept on stroking the material in front of her. But for the first time since coming to the department store she was oblivious to the sensation underneath her fingertips.

This Frau Lemke, Agatha had already noticed her the other day. The woman was taken by the royal-blue silk, and the pattern she returned to again and again showed an elegant, low-cut, knee-length cocktail dress. Agatha had noted Frau Lemke's good taste. The dress would show off her full figure and bust beautifully without looking vulgar. Instantly Agatha could interpret Frau Lemke's longing glances in the mirror, holding the silk against her body. Agatha now saw her in this blue dress sitting in an armchair, with an elegant champagne glass in one hand and a cigarette in the other, listening to a man playing a beautifully sad song on the violin.

'Guten Tag, Herr Lemke, my name is Frau Weiss.'

After much toing and froing in her head, she decided to stick to her real name. After all, she is hoping for more work afterwards, and it's highly unlikely that Herr Lemke will make the connection that she is Albert Lange's mother-in-law, not least because she has a different surname. Yes, Herr Lemke is the miller. But by the time Agatha had realized that – 'Lemke' is not an uncommon name – she had already started the preparations for today's visit.

'I am from the department store. Your wife asked for a dress sample.'

She opens her bag and takes out a little doll made of fabric that is wearing a miniature version of the blue silk dress. She stretches it out on her palm towards Herr Lemke. The doll has exactly the same proportions as his wife.

To obtain the fabric pieces for the doll and the dress was a challenge. Agatha had to steal. First she stole some scissors. A big strong pair. She hitchhiked to Hamburg and walked through the city for an entire day trying to find a suitable shop where there was a chance for her little theft to go unnoticed. She didn't want to steal from the department store because she would take the fabric from there. But as she walked through town she became aware that there were lots of other opportunities to get scrap material for the doll: she managed to sneak into a fancy hotel through the service door and grab a dirty towel out of a wash sack. A beige towel. She would use that for the skin of the doll. She cut a corner – a tiny corner – from a blanket on which a drunkard was sleeping. And eventually she found a sock floating in the gutter. By the time she went back that day, she had collected everything she needed for the doll. So all that was left for her to do at the department store was to cut a big enough piece of the royal-blue silk.

For a moment Herr Lemke looks confused, staring first at Agatha and then at the doll in her hand.

'My wife isn't here. She will be back in a couple of hours.'

Agatha expected that answer. After all, she had timed her

arrival so that she wouldn't bump into Frau Lemke. She has observed Frau Lemke and her house for two weeks and knows the woman's movements very well.

'Oh, what a pity.' Agatha once again smiles and looks straight at Herr Lemke, who is still looking at the doll. But now he's lifting his head. Agatha catches his eye.

'I'm sure you know that your wife has been looking at the fabric and pattern of this dress for weeks now.'

Agatha could feel that he was about to step back inside, wanting to bid her farewell.

She takes a deep breath. Everything so far has gone according to plan. So hopefully he will react to her next sentence as she has anticipated too.

She clears her throat. Also rehearsed.

'I can offer a very good rate and payment in instalments. All you would have to buy up front is the fabric and the thread.' She stretches out the hand holding the doll a couple of centimetres further towards him. But not too far. She can't appear pushy at this point.

She bought needles and thread – two reels: one blue for the dress and one beige for the doll's skin – with honest money. She also made sure that the grumpy manager was on duty, so he saw her walking up to the till and handing over the money. She wished she could tell him that it would work in his favour to be friendly to her – as a kind of future investment for his shop – because soon he'd get a lot of business through her.

Agatha has always been aware that this strategy could have only one of two outcomes. Either Herr Lemke will now slam the door in her face or he will be intrigued and engage her in conversation to find out more. The second reaction, however, is only possible if he loves his wife and would like to give her what she most desires: a new dress in which she might be able to seduce him. Up until the moment she knocked on the door, in fact up until this very moment, Agatha has always been convinced that the second outcome stands a good chance. He is clearly a sensitive man deep down, playing music and still mourning the loss of the son who died during the war. Even though, of course, he hides his feelings at the mill. Agatha is sure Albert doesn't know about this side of his employer.

'We do not buy from strangers.'

He steps back inside and closes the door before Agatha even has time to react. She is still standing there with her outstretched hand. Slowly she pulls her hand back and puts the doll into her bag. Then she turns and walks down the three steps. She misjudged the man. She shakes her head. She can't believe it. Her instinct for people is usually so right.

'Wait!'

She has reached the pavement. She looks over her shoulder. Herr Lemke has stepped outside the door, stands at the top of the stairs. 'Did you make the dress on the doll?'

Agatha's hand began to work its magic again. The dress for Frau Lemke proved a total success. Soon orders from her friends followed. And just before Christmas Agatha had made enough money to buy a sewing machine. Overnight, the store manager became her best friend.

In January of the new year, Trude and Albert were informed that their application for a two-bedroom flat in the new housing estate at the other end of town had been successful.

And so Trude, Albert, Peter and Agatha moved out of the camp in the spring.

In the meantime, Agatha's reputation was growing steadily. She asked Trude to stop the cleaning job and help her instead. 'We could make the same amount of money that way, and in due time even more,' Agatha pointed out. And suddenly, for the first time, Albert and Agatha found common ground. Because Albert, too, wanted Trude to hand in her notice, but for a different reason. Albert and Trude now had their own bedroom again – not yet with a double bed, but with a double mattress on the floor. Albert longed to fall asleep every evening with his wife in his arms, instead of waiting for her to slide under the covers at 3:30 in the morning after her shift.

Trude, however, continued with her cleaning job. She enjoyed the company of the women and would have missed her friend, Gerda. They were planning another dance show for the following summer.

The Boxing Match

T HE BOY IS electrified by the fight. Albert doesn't need to watch what is happening in the boxing ring. The spectacle is mirrored in his son's face. Each time his hero, Max Schmeling, gives his opponent, Walter Neusel, a hammering, Peter's face lights up, radiates, as his hands, formed into fists by his side, twitch in imitaton of Schmeling's successful hooks and punches or whatever you call them. Albert smiles to himself.

'Did you see that, Dad, did you see that!'

Peter briefly turns his face towards his father and then back again. He doesn't want to miss anything. This is the best day of his life. He still can't believe he is here. Every now and then he opens his fist and pinches himself on the thigh to make sure, doubly sure, triply sure, that he's awake and not dreaming.

'Dad! Look at his ringcraft. Neusel stands no chance. No cha—'

Peter stops mid-word. He stares, mouth open, forgets to breathe, scrunches up his face. His head jerks backwards. His hero must be under attack.

When the posters about the fight went up, Albert got the tickets straight away. Didn't think twice about it. A spur-of-the-moment decision. Cost him an arm and a leg.

He pushed his hat back as he walked in and laid the two

tickets on the kitchen table in front of his son. They had moved into the two-bedroom flat two months ago.

'Want to come with me, son?'

Peter looked at the tickets, looked at his father. Then looked at the tickets again. Since the smashing of the trophy, they had both stuck to their sides of the deal. In a manly, taciturn fashion. Peter humours Albert by going for walks with him during which his father talks about photography and they pretend to take photos. But so far Peter knows that Albert hasn't put any film inside the camera. At the same time, Peter continues with his boxing and stays out of trouble with the local boys. Albert, in turn, hasn't said a word against Peter's boxing again, but neither has he turned up to watch.

Albert pushed his hat back even further. He should have taken it off – and would do in a moment. But for the time being it made him feel better, more in control, keeping it on. Because he felt embarrassed. Embarrassed about wanting to take his son to the fight. After all these months of wanting Peter to stop. But Albert knows Max Schmeling. Met him. Yes, indeed. As he caught a glimpse of the poster advertising Schmeling and Neuser's big comeback fight, it struck him like a bolt of lightning. He had forgotten. Even watched Schmeling's biggest defeat almost to the day ten years ago in Hamburg. And he had talked to him.

'You talked to him?'

Peter didn't dare touch the tickets that were still lying in front of him on the table.

Albert scratched his forehead underneath the hat, then sat down opposite his son at the table. He was relieved that neither Agatha nor Trude were at home and he had caught his son on his own. Made things at least a bit easier.

'Well . . . I saw him get out of his car – before the fight. There was a big crowd of us. And I raised my camera and shouted, "After the fight?" And he lifted his thumb in my direction and nodded.'

'Wow!' Peter's throat was dry. He hadn't swallowed since his father had placed the tickets in front of him. 'He looked at you! Schmeling looked at you!'

Albert nodded, then finally took off his hat and wiped the sweat from his forehead.

Peter was impressed. And told everyone at the club. How his father even shook hands with Max Schmeling. The boy made that up, of course. But they could have, couldn't they, shaken hands, his dad and Schmeling? They were close enough. And everything else between Schmeling and his dad really happened. Finally Peter had a story, a really good story, to tell about his dad.

'So what does it feel like when you are there in the ring, facing your opponent?'

Albert and Peter are sitting in a café, Albert with a beer and Peter with a lemonade. Schmeling lost after twelve rounds. Albert expected Peter to be down, not least because the defeat means that this was Schmeling's last fight. He announced before the fight that if he lost he would retire from professional boxing. But Peter doesn't seem to mind.

'He's quite old, you know. Forty-two. And he did a good job coming back to professional boxing after the war,' he mused as they were leaving the Sportplatz in Altona. 'Schmeling felt that he had to. The sport needed role models to get back on to its feet.'

Again Albert smiled to himself. Peter sounded like a

semi-professional sports commentator. They must have discussed Schmeling and the ins and outs of his career at the boxing club non-stop in the last few weeks.

Peter now sips his lemonade through a straw. He wishes this day would never end. He leans back, looks his father in the eyes.

'The loneliest man on earth is the boxer when he hears the bell. That's what my trainer always says. And it's true. Because from that moment on, no one can help you.'

'Do you like this feeling?' Albert would love to lean across the table, give his son a hug and tell him that he isn't alone. No longer.

Peter shrugs and sucks on the straw again. 'I just like boxing.'

For a while neither say a word. Suddenly Peter lifts his head: 'Do you want to come and watch me next Saturday?' The moment the question is out he feels the heat rising. He shouldn't have done that.

'I'll do that,' Albert says.

The light of the street lamps throws yellow circles on to the pavement. Peter has to step right into the middle of each one without his feet touching the contours, while keeping step with his father, who doesn't know about this rule and mustn't find out about it either. If Peter doesn't manage to step into one of the circles, or if his father finds out, this day will remain an exception and he and his dad will never spend another nice day together. And even more, his father will change his mind and not watch him boxing. That's the deal Peter has struck with fate.

They haven't spoken since they got off the bus. But it's

not an awkward silence. A mild, early-summer night's calm, Albert thinks as he takes another drag on his cigarette. For a moment he puts his free hand on Peter's shoulder. But immediately he feels the boy tense, so he takes it away again. He's aware that Peter is playing a game with himself. And he's also aware that Peter thinks his father doesn't know. That's probably part of the game. Albert doesn't want to disturb it. He takes another pull on his cigarette and turns his head slightly upwards. Perfect smoke rings escape from his mouth and ascend into the night sky.

Next to him, Peter has started humming a melody. Albert throws him a glance. Peter is concentrating on his steps. The humming is soft. He's probably not even aware of it.

A familiar melody. So familiar. Albert hasn't heard it for a long time, resurfacing from the depths of memory. *Hang him from the lamppost. Hang him from the lamppost. Your own Lili Marleen.* Peter is now gently singing the words.

Albert's heart misses a beat.

He drops the cigarette butt, buries both hands in his trouser pockets. He watches Peter's feet out of the corner of his eye to make sure the boy is winning his game. Every now and again he imperceptibly adjusts his steps so as not to disturb his son's rhythm while keeping in line with him.

They turn into their street. Peter lifts his gaze. He's won. He's succeeded. Each time his feet landed perfectly inside the light circle. He can now relax. There will be other nice days with his dad. Peter looks at his father who is walking next to him, hands in pockets, hat on his forehead, slightly bent forward, lost in thought.

Suddenly his father turns his face and smiles.

'You were humming a very old song there.'

Peter's face brightens like the moon hanging above them. 'Do you remember? Mum and you used to dance to it secretly at night. Sometimes I watched you through the crack of the door.'

'Yes, I remember.'

They have reached the front door of their building.

'We should do this again, have another outing, don't you think?' Albert says, putting his arm around his son's shoulder and very quickly pulling the boy close to him.

The Photographer

T RUDE IS CYCLING ahead. It's the first hot day of the
summer and she is too excited about her own bicycle to
wait for Albert, who is stopping every now and again.

'I will go on and come back,' she says, laughing against the
wind. 'And if we miss each other I will wait at the dyke for
you.' She waves.

Albert slows down. He's passing a turning into a side road,
and just at that moment two boys about Peter's age shoot
around the corner on their bikes, nearly crashing into Albert.

'Sorry,' they mumble without looking up, racing off in the
direction from where Albert and Trude have just come.

Albert had to jump off his bike in order to prevent a crash.
He looks down the side road, a cul-de-sac with only one
derelict building still standing and the road pretty much re-
claimed by nature. There is a track made by the boys' bicycle
wheels, leading through the weeds towards the building. He
focuses his camera. There is film inside, but he doesn't press
the button. Instead he follows the trail. Multiple footprints
through the grass draw him to the back of the building. There
is a little fireplace with logs placed around it in a circle. Clearly
a boys' hang-out. Albert smiles. At the front he rests his bicycle
against a tree trunk. Debris crunches underfoot as he walks
through the ground floor. He halts. No sounds. The birds
have stopped singing too. This must have been a warehouse.
Empty metal shelves hang from the walls, but otherwise it

has been totally cleaned out. Albert throws a quick glance down the cellar stairs. He spots a couple of ropes lying on the floor. As he straightens up a cold shiver runs down his spine. The sweat from cycling has dried and turned into a chilly membrane on his skin.

Outside, the warm air strokes his naked arms where he's rolled up his sleeves.

He catches up with Trude by the small harbour. It's high tide. They timed their swim well. This time they checked the tide table in the newspaper before heading out. Not like last year, when they didn't know about the big tidal differences of the North Sea. Cutters and small fishing boats are dancing on the glittering water. Some are decorated with streamers of red and yellow and blue and white and orange flags. Trude is sitting on a bench, her legs stretched out in front of her, her face turned towards the sun. Her bicycle is standing next to her.

'I thought you couldn't wait because you just had to keep on cycling,' he teases her.

'A shrimp cutter has just come in,' she says with a smile, squinting up at him. 'We could eat them after our swim.'

And then down the dyke they race again. This time on their own bikes. Trude's hair and dress - her new summer dress, green with white daisies; fabric Agatha got on the cheap, her first summer dress in six years - flutter in the wind.

At the bottom of the dyke, they look left and right. No one in sight. They undress quickly down to their underwear and clamber over the rocks and into the water. Albert throws himself backwards into the glittering sea, disappearing for a moment. He's back up, drops flying away from him in all directions, and he grasps the shrieking Trude and pulls her down with him and kisses her under the water – a beautiful salty kiss.

Albert swims out towards the horizon, front crawl, back crawl, breaststroke. Every muscle in his body is moving. For fun.

Trude is dozing on her back in the grass. Albert towels himself dry, then lies down with his head on her stomach. A couple of seagulls are screeching up above. Trude's right hand lazily strokes Albert's hair. She wonders if the seagulls have smelled the bag of shrimps and are now waiting for the feast. Her eyes close. She feels that she is about to drift off to sleep.

'It was Peter who knew about the Black Radio, wasn't it?'

Albert has put his left arm across his face in such a way that if he opens his eyes he can still see the glittering sea. He opens, squeezes, opens, squeezes his eyes in quick succession, taking snapshots. He used to play that game for entire afternoons out by the Madüsee, lying belly down on the wooden jetty. He never got bored of it. Each snapshot was different. Revealed a different star formation on the water.

For a moment Trude's consciousness hovers on the threshold of darkness and sleep further down, and the sun and the blue sky and her hand on Albert's head if she decides to stay awake. She knows she could go either way.

She opens her eyes. The seagulls are still there, hovering, their heads to one side, looking right down at them.

'Yes.'

She waits for the next question about her mother. Albert surely has made that connection too.

He has.

He takes his arm from his eyes, lifts his head from Trude's

stomach, turns so that he is now lying right next to her. He places his head on her shoulder. Her wet hair on his cheek. He smells the salt in it. Trude closes her eyes again.

After a while, Albert sits up. A cutter is heading back to the harbour, white bow waves at the front and a white cloud of gulls following at the back. He fetches his camera.

She feels his lips on hers. Then he whispers, 'Smile,' and turns to lie down again next to her, temple against temple, holding the camera above them with his outstretched arm.

Click.

NEW BOOKS FROM SALT

XAN BROOKS
The Clocks in This House All Tell Different Times
(978-1-78463-093-5)

RON BUTLIN
Billionaires' Banquet (978-1-78463-100-0)

MICKEY J CORRIGAN
Project XX (978-1-78463-097-3)

MARIE GAMESON
The Giddy Career of Mr Gadd (deceased) (978-1-78463-118-5)

LESLEY GLAISTER
The Squeeze (978-1-78463-116-1)

NAOMI HAMILL
How To Be a Kosovan Bride (978-1-78463-095-9)

CHRISTINA JAMES
Fair of Face (978-1-78463-108-6)

SIMON KINCH
Two Sketches of Disjointed Happiness (978-1-78463-110-9)

STEFAN MOHAMED
Stanly's Ghost (978-1-78463-076-8)

EMILY MORRIS
My Shitty Twenties (978-1-78463-091-1)

SIMON OKOTIE
In the Absence of Absalon (978-1-78463-102-4)

NICHOLAS ROYLE (ed.)
Best British Short Stories 2017 (978-1-78463-112-3)

GUY WARE
Reconciliation (978-1-78463-104-8)

TONY WILLIAMS
Nutcase (978-1-78463-106-2)

MEIKE ZIERVOGEL
The Photographer (978-1-78463-114-7)

RECENT FICTION FROM SALT

GERRI BRIGHTWELL
Dead of Winter (978-1-78463-049-2)

NEIL CAMPBELL
Sky Hooks (978-1-78463-037-9)

DAVID GAFFNEY
More Sawn-Off Tales (978-1-78463-099-7)

SUE GEE
Trio (978-1-78463-061-4)

CHRISTINA JAMES
Rooted in Dishonour (978-1-78463-089-8)

V.H. LESLIE
Bodies of Water (978-1-78463-071-3)

ROBIN INCE, JOHNNY MAINS (eds.)
Dead Funny: Encore (978-1-78463-039-3)

WYL MENMUIR
The Many (978-1-78463-048-5)

ALSO AVAILABLE FROM SALT

ELIZABETH BAINES
Too Many Magpies (978-1-84471-721-7)
The Birth Machine (978-1-907773-02-0)

LESLEY GLAISTER
Little Egypt (978-1-907773-72-3)

ALISON MOORE
The Lighthouse (978-1-907773-17-4)
The Pre-War House and Other Stories (978-1-907773-50-1)
He Wants (978-1-907773-81-5)
Death and the Seaside (978-1-78463-069-0)

ALICE THOMPSON
Justine (978-1-78463-031-7)
The Falconer (978-1-78463-009-6)
The Existential Detective (978-1-78463-011-9)
Burnt Island (978-1-907773-48-8)
The Book Collector (978-1-78463-043-0)

This book has been typeset by
SALT PUBLISHING LIMITED
using Neacademia, a font designed by Sergei Egorov
for the Rosetta Type Foundry in the Czech Republic.
It is manufactured using Creamy 70gsm, a Forest
Stewardship Council™ certified paper from Stora Enso's
Anjala Mill in Finland. It was printed and bound by
Clays Limited in Bungay, Suffolk, Great Britain.

LONDON
GREAT BRITAIN
MMXVII